In Case of
Unexpected Hazards

I0520491

Keith Pitsch

Popple Lake Press

Dedication

To Rick, Mark, and Todd and to the spirit of all the Good Guys and the great north woods.

Acknowledgments

Thanks to my wonderful critique group of Sylvia Acevedo, Valerie Biel, and Christine Esser and to my wife, Roxann who never let me stop believing.

Contents

IN CASE OF UNEXPECTED HAZARDS

Prologue: Under the Elms

Once there were elm trees, great silent friends who protected us from searing sun and chilling rain. On warm summer nights their leaves whispered and murmured, telling each other tales of the events they witnessed below. In low voices they sang of heroic deeds unknown to most of the world, but their songs moved those who understood.

Sometimes it seems like it happened in another life, another time. It was a happy time, yet a time of danger, but danger to face and overcome. It was a time few now remember, but even for them, memory flickers and fades. Our hearts believed that summer would never end: neither the summer of earth and sun, nor the summer of our youths. We played, explored the pasture and woods of the farm, or just sat on the front porch of our grandparents' house, drinking green Kool-Aid and watching the river flow by as we planned our next adventure. We had our chores, but we also had hours of freedom to spend in a world of natural beauty with a magic of its own. We had, at least for the summer, each other.

When night fell, our other lives began, our secret lives. Then our strange friends visited, arriving in large groups, covering the lawn. Soon unwanted visitors appeared, and we fought to drive them away. We believed then, in our faithful hearts, that we could ultimately defeat them, that we could save the world from Unexpected Hazards. It was another time, this time of adventure, but not so long ago.

Adventures we had. They seemed never to end, only to pause long enough for us to catch our breaths before another began. The elm trees could have sung their tales for a year and a day and still not have finished. But they are gone now and can never tell.

Chapter 1: Hands

The six companions stood in the gathering dusk of the forest. Before them loomed their enemies' headquarters. This was the last place they wanted to be, a place where they might be outnumbered by a hundred to one or worse. Not only must they be there, but in a few moments they would be entering that evil fortress.

If they had known that leering eyes stared at them even then, would they have held to their plans? Had they known that news of their approach had already gone into that dark structure, would they have reconsidered? Had they known the wicked welcome being prepared for them, would they have fled?

Full darkness filled the forest. The company advanced. Keith thought again of a bright morning just over three days ago.

Keith rose early that morning, too excited to sleep longer. Looking about, he remembered that he was not in his own room but in his grandparents' house. He heard the quiet breathing of his three cousins, just in from California and sleeping peacefully. He lived for those weeks in the summer when they came to stay on the farm, and he had planned a big day. It would be, but not as he expected.

In those days, a Wisconsin farm boy like Keith had a limited number of ways to spend his leisure time, assuming he got his chores done promptly enough to have any. He might go fishing. He might bike to a friend's house. He might play little league baseball or try out for the town team when he grew older as Keith, now 15, looked forward to next year. In either case, games and practices only filled a few hours of two or three days in the week. Other organized activities came and went quickly and none too often, so having fun demanded a certain amount of creativity and effort. Nothing, however, compared with having cousins visit.

The winter before, inspiration struck Keith. He would build a golf course in the pasture. Long before the snow melted, he sketched a layout. When the thaw and early spring rains softened the earth, he sunk nine tin cans into the ground, carefully covering each with a rock, lest a cow should step in it and get hurt. The herd of forty or so Jersey cows and yearling heifers were, after all, his head greens keepers, a delicious job in their opinion. They did tend to leave a few hazards of their own around the course, but farm kids learned early to step lightly around such obstacles.

Keith had a small supply of golf balls that he had found here and there over the years, but he had no clubs. At first he used a gnarled tag-alder stem with an enlargement at one end. Although sturdy, its club face was not what you might call perfectly flat, and even a solidly struck drive might fly in any number of directions. Frustrated, Keith sought a better solution. Soon he landed upon the idea of drilling a hole in a two-by-four scrap and wedging the end of a broomstick into it. This innovation produced a much more consistent result despite the club head's tendency to fly off the broomstick and outdistance the ball. All in all, however, the whole system made for a game that resembled real golf, and Keith spent many hours enjoying it.

Today would be a golf day. Keith nudged Rick, his oldest cousin, only younger than himself by a month. Rick yawned and rubbed his hands through his rusty hair, which, along with a generous splash of freckles, gave him the look of Tom Sawyer awakening. His second oldest cousin, Mark, presented more of a challenge. Almost thirteen, he loved sleeping well into the morning. When ear tickling and singing goofy wakeup songs failed, they shook his bed until he sat up, grumbling. They decided to let nine-year-old Todd sleep. How many times in the days to come would they wish they had done the same for Mark?

Dressing quickly, they bounded downstairs and ate a breakfast of eggs fried by their grandmother. Gathering their golf equipment, they walked south from the farmhouse past the buildings that squeezed between the river to the east and a steep hill to the west. Most of the farm, with its hills, fields, woods, open pastures, and hidden valleys, spread out atop and beyond that hill. A creek, "the crick," whose two branches merged on the north end of the farm cut through it from north to south.

They passed the woodshed, the chicken coop, and the garage. As they walked down the driveway, the river glinted through the trees on their left. To their right, the leaves of the lilacs, so recently filled with blossoms, rustled gently. They passed a corncrib and entered the barn. A half dozen Jersey calves lifted their heads to watch the boys file past. Seeing them for the first time, the California cousins stopped to scratch each one's head.

They emerged from the barn and picked their way across the barnyard, following a cow trail behind Keith's house and past the machine shed. The foundation of an old inn marked the spot where the trail began to climb along the hillside for a thousand feet or so until it rounded a corner. Here the hill nearly flattened out in a meadow stretching to the south while rising northward to the summit in a field they knew as Buckwheat Hill.

In the distance, the drone of a tractor rose and fell. Somewhere on the river below, the whine of motors grew stronger as boats approached from downriver—fishermen, no doubt.

Keith looked to the meadow as it gently sloped away from him. He teed up a golf ball and aimed for the first green, perched on a point where the land fell off sharply as the crick on the west bent to join the river on the east. His drive bounced along the rough ground, kicked off a large stone, and lodged next to a gooseberry bush at the edge of the east bank. Rick followed with an impressive shot that rolled to a stop a good fifty feet beyond where his club head landed.

They turned to Mark who picked up his club and dropped it abruptly. "I can't swing," he said.

"Not as well as me," Rick replied. "That's obvious. It never stopped you before, though. So hurry up."

"I mean I *can't* swing. I've got a hanny."

"A what?" asked Keith.

"A hanny. You know, like when your hands really bug you when you try to grip anything? Ew, I can't hold onto this thing."

"Come on, Mark. Don't be stupid," said Rick.

"No. I really can't yet. You guys go ahead. I'll catch up."

Rick and Keith rolled their eyes at each other and at Mark before proceeding down the fairway. Keith, however, whispered to Rick, "I've had that happen."

Finishing the first hole, they drove back toward the second green, which lay next to the first tee. When they got there they spotted Mark half asleep on a patch of moss beneath a towering oak tree, his dark brown hair hanging halfway over his eyes.

"Are you ever going to get started, Mark?" asked Rick.

"I'm just about ready." He flexed his hands. "Just a couple more minutes and I should be okay. I'll catch up. One person alone can move pretty fast."

"Sure, if he can hit the ball straight," said Rick. "All right. Just don't dawdle. You're really getting carried away with this hanny thing."

Rick and Keith finished the second hole and moved to the third tee. Its fairway dropped off steeply into a small glen carved by the crick. On the glen's flat surface, about thirty feet below the level of the tee, the green nestled next to the stream. Rick and Keith looked to Mark before descending into the flat, but he showed no signs of motion. With another roll of the eyes, they ran to the green, criss-crossing the hillside to avoid tumbling out of control.

Holing out, they made their fourth drives, tricky shots that had to clear the crick. Their own crossing was just as tricky, but as they hopped from rock to rock, they felt the freedom only known to schoolboys in June. Could life be better?

Just as Keith was about to suggest that they sit by the crick and wait for Mark, raucous voices disturbed the peace. Something had riled a group of crows. The birds scolded and quarreled with everything and everyone nearby, and they showed no signs of ceasing. "Did you know that a flock of crows is called a murder?" asked Keith.

"No wonder," said Rick. "It sounds like a crime going on."

Did Keith notice, far in the background, voices equally unpleasant as the crows'? If so, he paid it no heed and passed it off as part of the birds' general squabbling. At length, the flock flew up the crick, and tranquility returned. But was that some kind of echo in the distance?

Rick and Keith finished the ninth hole without further incident. Mark still had not caught them. "He's probably looking for a lost ball or something," Rick said.

They joked back and forth with each other about their play and the state of Mark's game as they retraced the holes. By the time they reached the third hole and still saw no sign of Mark, their joking ceased. Exchanging nervous glances, they climbed to the third tee. Once there, they scanned the first two holes and saw nothing.

"He must have gone home," said Keith.

"No, look!" Rick shouted and pointed toward the first tee. A club still leaned against the oak tree. They ran to the tree and saw tees and balls scattered along a line leading down the first fairway. Following this trail they reached a spot where the brush at the side of the hill lay trampled to the ground. At first Keith thought the cows might have done the damage, but a closer look at the cracked and broken branches and the flattened grass beyond convinced him otherwise.

"Bad Guys!" he shouted with a gasp.

Mark was gone.

Chapter 2: Plans

Rick and Keith plunged down the hill, heedless of the grasping brush that scratched their arms and tore at their pants. The Bad Guys had chosen their route through a patch of prickly ash, an unpleasant shrub with short but very sharp thorns. Emerging from the tangle, Rick and Keith had little trouble following the trail through the grass beyond. The Bad Guys obviously had taken no care to disguise their route, but when it reached the river, it vanished abruptly.

"They must have waded upstream or down to throw us off!" Rick cried.

"Or swam across. Or had a boat." Keith knew this enemy well. He had fought them for years and had brought his cousins into the Good Guys. *I should have known better than to leave Mark alone.*

Waving his arms wildly, Rick took several steps upstream, scanned the shoreline, and took several more steps. "You go downriver and see if you can pick up a trail. I'll go this way," he called over his shoulder as he stumbled along the rocky bank.

Keith shouted his agreement and turned southwards. At first, he ran easily along a path that fishermen had worn beside the river. He reached the mouth of the crick and picked his way across it on exposed rocks. Now the bank steepened sharply, and in some spots prickly ash clustered down to the water, forcing him to wade around it. His tennis shoes slipped and skidded along rocks covered with a green slime.

When the bank finally leveled off, he found another fishermen's trail that merged with a cow path, and he followed it with renewed speed. Once, he jumped and slid to a halt as a water snake slithered across his way and splashed into the river. When he resumed, he watched the snake keeping pace with him as it swam downstream, its head thrust above the surface. Keith found himself watching not only for signs of the kidnappers, but also for any other creatures in his path.

The trail ended all too soon, forcing him to plow on through tall, sharp swamp grass, which hid numerous rocks, fallen logs, and tussocks. His progress slowed as he tripped and stumbled along, trying to avoid the obstacles. All the while, one thing remained constant—he saw no sign of Bad Guys or Mark.

After about half a mile he came to a marshy slough that completely halted his progress. With a last look downstream, he retraced his steps, hoping that Rick's luck had been better. By the time he reached the starting point, he was breathing heavily, and his knee bled from an encounter with a hidden rock. Not seeing Rick, he continued upstream until he found him seated on a log, his head in his hands.

Rick looked up, and Keith saw a hopeful look turn to despair. "We've got to swim across," Rick shouted. He lurched to the bank and waded in, only to fall head first into the stream when a loose stone gave way beneath his feet. Before he could right himself, Keith grabbed his arm. Jerking away, Rick screamed, "What are you doing? Let go."

"We can't do it this way. It's too late."

"No! Let me go." Rick wrenched himself away, and they both toppled into the river with a great splash. Keith regained his footing first. He pulled Rick up and clasped him around the waist, pinning his arms against his sides.

"Rick, this is no good. We'll probably find nothing over there, and then all we'd have done is waste more time. What if they had a boat? We need to get some help. Maybe one of our scouts saw something. Think like a Good Guy, not just a brother. Panic will get us nowhere."

At last Rick relaxed. He shook his head and slapped his hip. "All right," he said.

They hurried up the bank and emerged from the trees where another faded fieldstone foundation, once the site of a long-forgotten barn, burrowed into the hill. Rounding a slight bend, the farm came into sight as they passed the inn's foundation. They jogged past the machine shed, Keith's house, the little barn, the main barn, and up the hill to the great white farmhouse where their grandparents lived.

Huffing and puffing, they ran into the kitchen and found Todd eating a bowl of cereal. "Where's Mark?" he asked. "How come you guys are all wet?"

Jabbing an elbow into Keith's side, Rick answered. "We fell in the crick. Mark's still out there." He led Keith into the living room and whispered, "Let's see what we can find out before we get him all worried. You make a few calls, and I'll talk to Todd."

Rick returned to find Todd finishing the cereal. "Would you like me to make you some toast?" Rick asked.

"No. Grandma made me an egg and toast before she and Mom went to get groceries. So why didn't Mark come with you guys?"

Rick walked to the sink and stared out the window above it, keeping his face turned away from Todd. "He...isn't done...golfing yet."

"How come you sound funny, Rick?" Todd was only nine years old, but he had already started his Good Guy training. Under his shock of thick, blonde hair worked an unusually sharp brain.

"Maybe I'm still cold from falling in the water."

Todd decided not to press the issue. "Do you want to play with the dinosaurs?" he asked, referring to a set of figurines he had arranged into family groups on the table.

"I can't. I think Keith and I are going to go out to the golf course and do a little work on it...with Mark, of course."

"I'll help."

Rick turned from the window. "No. You need to stay here. You can, uh, let Mom know where we are when she gets back. Besides, we might have to do some Good Guy stuff."

"But I'm a Good Guy."

"Maybe later. Remember, you have to tell Mom."

"I don't want to stay here alone," Todd protested.

"But you're not alone," said a high-pitched voice from above him.

Todd looked up and saw a small head peeking out from the light fixture. "Good morning, George," he said.

A tiny arm waved back. Whatever George was, he had lived in the electric circuits of Grandpa and Grandma's house as long as anyone could remember. He was not very big, but he was what one might describe as wiry. He could travel easily through the circuits, but he rarely traveled far from them. A longtime Good Guy, his wit was lightning quick, and he packed a powerful punch. No one knew quite what he was or where he came from, but his special talents, his faithful service, and his constant cheerfulness made him a valuable and beloved ally. "I'll keep you company, Todd," he squeaked.

"All right," said Todd. He looked at Rick. "As soon as you guys get ready to do something fun, let me know."

Keith returned to the room and motioned to Rick. "We have to go now."

With a wave to Todd and George, they opened the door, only to hear the "pop, pop, pop" of an old-fashioned car engine. Keith peeked out the opening and saw a rickety, red Model A pickup pulling into the driveway. "Oh, no. It's Dr. Rankato."

Todd sprang up, his eyes wide. "Is he a Bad Guy?"

Keith shook his head. "No. Far from it. He's perfectly harmless. You can talk to him as long as you want. Just don't buy anything from him. Come on, Rick. We don't have time for this." They slipped out the back door, just as the pickup chugged to a halt out front.

Hearing knocking at the front door, Todd asked George if he should answer it. When George signaled with an upraised thumb, he opened the door and saw a curious figure standing on the mat. It was that of an old man, at least old to Todd. He wore an ill-fitting checked suit with an oversized polka dotted bowtie and a hat to match the suit. His bushy, white mustache partially hid a pleasant, and almost sincere, smile.

He tipped his hat to Todd. "Good morning, young fellow. Dr. Rankato at your service with all the goods to meet all your needs. That's Rankato, as in Mankato. Is your mother home?"

"No, sir."

"Never mind, never mind. I might have just the things you need for yourself. How about this tin can polisher? No home should be without one. If you have a tin can handy, I'll be happy to demonstrate."

Todd shook his head.

"No problem. It's not what you were probably looking for, anyhow. Could I interest you in these right- and left-footed shoelaces? They are color coded, so never again will you have to wonder which lace goes in which shoe. No, never again will you suffer the embarrassment of having your friends spot you with the wrong lace in the wrong shoe."

Todd lifted up one bare foot.

"Perhaps you are looking for a stylish fashion accessory. How about one of these rat-tailed bow ties? They are all the rage in Europe. I just managed to save this boxful from a huge shipment we sent over to Venezuela. I tell you those Europeans are sharp dressers. If you want to be a trendsetter, you must have one of these. I'll let one go for the low, low introductory price of fifty cents because I know that once you get one, you will surely be back for more."

Todd shrugged.

"You look like the kind of guy who keeps a goldfish. Maybe a pet guppy. If so, you can't go wrong with an eight-pack of fish diapers. People have been clamoring for them for years, but they were held up by red tape at the Albanian patent office. That's why they fasten with these little pieces of red tape. These are the first prototypes available. You can't get them in stores yet."

"The first what?"

"Then again, you might just be looking for one of these...."

Rick and Keith sneaked out the back door and crept away from the house behind a line of bushes. When they reached the last bush, they parted its branches and looked back at the house. Seeing that Dr. Rankato was busy talking to Todd, they dashed the last few feet to the garage. Safely out of sight, they passed the barn and started down a cow path.

A moment later, Keith signaled Rick to stop. On a hunch, he ran to his mailbox and opened it. He drew a white envelope out and stuffed it in his back pocket.

All along their trip to the pasture, the world went on as if nothing was different from any other day. Sunlight still glinted off the river. The power plant across the stream in Vermillion Falls hummed its usual song. Rounding the corner on Buckwheat Hill, they saw Keith's father mowing the hay, and their noses filled with its sweet smell. Keith's dad waved at them from the tractor, and they waved back.

Yet nothing felt normal to them. The crick's rippling and gurgling sounded less like merry laughter than usual. The bird's voices resembled squabbling more than singing. The "cooee-coo-

coo-coo" of the mourning dove set a melancholy mood. They walked on, each deep in thought.

Passing the last holes of the golf course, they came to a heavily wooded section of the pasture on the south end of a field. The "front field," one of the two largest on the farm, stretched hundreds of yards to the north. Near the top, it bent around to the west and turned south like a backward letter h. Inside its loop, tall white pines, oaks, birches and butternut trees hid a valley known as Dead Man's Gulch. Its steep, tree-lined slopes made it one of the most secluded places on the farm.

Winding to the bottom of the gulch, they came to an ancient pine where they sat down on a mossy tuft. They waited several minutes before two figures approached from the other direction. The one on the right advanced with clenched fists that, when opened, exposed claws at the ends of hairy fingers. His broad back and barrel chest shook with rage, and sharp fangs flashed as he growled, "Filthy swine."

The other, almost equally burly, reached out and gripped a hairy arm in his hand. "Patience, Marc," he said. He then shook his huge head, and a mane of thin, blonde hair whipped from side to side.

At that moment, they spotted Keith and Rick. The hairy one rushed to Rick, gave him a powerful hug, and whispered, "We won't stop until we get him back." Then Marc Monster stepped back, and Rick saw a tear in his eye.

Perhaps because of sharing the name (almost), or perhaps because of the many times he had tutored Mark in his early years, Marc Monster felt a special bond with the young fellow. He was not someone that anyone would want to rile up, and he was riled at the Bad Guys.

"How ya doin', folks?" said the other. The sad look on his face told them that this was more a greeting than a question.

"Not so well," said Rick. "But thanks for being here, Lugu. Is this everyone?"

"Nope, we're here, too," rang a voice from the woods on the left. A short man stepped out from behind a tree. A smile crossed everyone's face despite the somberness of the occasion. Happiness Bowdy had that affect on people. A scarecrow and a caveman followed him from the woods and greeted Rick and Keith.

"This is all we could round up on such short notice," said Satch Scarecrow. "Friendly Doctor was visiting us, or he never could have been here," he continued, placing his hand on the caveman's shoulder.

Keith waited until everyone settled in. "Thank you for coming today. We probably should get started. You all know why I called you here. The Bad Guys have taken Mark, and we need to come up with a plan."

"How much plan do we need?" said Marc Monster. "What we need is to get all the Good Guys together and march on Bad Guy headquarters as soon as possible." Some of the others nodded and growled in approval. Rick shrugged and looked thoughtfully into the woods.

Keith raised his hand to interrupt Marc who looked ready to charge out and rouse the troops immediately. He tried not to look at Rick but couldn't help sending a glance his way. "Before we do anything hasty, I think we should think things out. For one thing, I have something here we should read."

He reached into his back pocket and pulled out the envelope he had found in the mailbox. It bore neither stamp nor return address. The only marks on it were the words "GUD GY" in crudely printed letters.

He opened it, pulled out a badly folded page, and read aloud.

"Gud Gy, we've got your brat. If you ever want to see him again, you better do like we say. First, don't mess with our operations. Stay out of our way, or he gets it. We'll kep an eye on

you fer a cuppl of weeks until Lootenant's Day, and then we'll let you
know what comes next. That's provided you lay off us. You get
that?"

Keith lowered the page and looked at the faces of his friends.
No one spoke for some time. They all knew about Lieutenant's Day.
It was one of the biggest of Bad Guy holidays. It dated from the
Civil War days when Unexpected Hazards roamed the country with a
band of renegades, deserters from both armies. The gang's leader, a
Confederate lieutenant, had been a ruthless brigand. One day,
heavily under the influence of stolen whiskey, he began firing his
pistols into the air…and behind his back into his own troops.
Unexpected Hazards and several other renegades became so enraged
that they deserted from the deserters. They made their way north to
what is now Bad Guy Country and set up shop. As much as the Bad
Guys hated the lieutenant, they celebrated the anniversary of their
breakaway from him, the day of the founding of their order, and it
was to this day they referred in the letter.

After letting the meaning set in, Keith continued. He related
what had occurred on the golf course. Then he concluded. "Here's a
few other facts I got when I called our scouts. Then I'll let Rick take
over. Our scouts tell me they saw a group of about a half-dozen
BadGuys a couple of miles downriver from this farm. Apparently,

they stole two motorboats from the Wild Duck Resort and headed north faster than our scouts could follow on foot. The next time they were spotted, they had abandoned the boats and were hurrying north toward Bad Guy Country, driving Mark along with them. That's what we know other than what's in the note I read. No one knows who dropped that off."

He sat down, and Rick stepped forward. He spoke slowly at first. "After hearing what the note says, I don't think we should rush into an all-out assault. I'm guessing that we have some time, and if we attack, who knows what they might do to Mark. I think you would agree, Marc.

"Still, we can't just sit back and let them have free rein with their 'operations.' We need to protect the farms, homes, cabins and people living in and around Bad Guy Country. So we need to act quickly but not too obviously. We have to lull them into believing we are doing what they say while making our move sudden before they can react and harm my brother. It looks like we have about two weeks. I'd like to get something done sooner, but that's definitely our limit."

"Can we talk freely?" asked Satch Scarecrow. "We don't want to be overheard."

"We can," said Keith. "Our scouts have scoured the perimeter of the gulch, and they'll let us know if spies come around."

The group fell into a long discussion. After listing many options and voicing many suggestions, they decided that the best plan would be to send a small party to spirit Mark away from the Bad Guys. This brought up a number of other issues: how to set off without being missed, how to reach Bad Guy headquarters without being seen, how to find Mark once they got there, how to get him out and get back safely. Most importantly, who should go.

The debate went on well into the afternoon until a workable plan emerged. They dispersed with orders to assemble a mass meeting of the Good Guys that night at Buckwheat Hill. Rick and Keith left just in time to bring the cows home for the evening milking. Rick immediately returned to Buckwheat Hill where the Lugu and Marc Monster waited.

For now, Keith had the tough job of explaining their upcoming absence. Although hating to lie to the family, he had no choice. He told them that they had planned a camping and fishing trip to last for a few days. Rick and Mark were setting up the campsite, he said. Todd would be staying home.

Dealing with Todd was a tougher task. "I want to go, too," he demanded.

"We've already planned it."

"But how much difference would one person make?"

"I told your mom you wouldn't be going."

"Mom won't mind."

"We have a Good Guy meeting, too."

"I'm a Good Guy. Listen, I know something is up, and I'm old enough and ready enough to handle it. I could tell by the way Rick acted today that there is some kind of problem. If I am ever to be a full-fledged Good Guy, I need to start sooner or later, and sooner is now."

Keith didn't answer for a minute or two. Todd kept his eyes on him, pleading. At last Keith said, "All right. You can come to the meeting." Todd's eyes persisted. "And maybe on the camping trip or at least part of it."

"Neat," said Todd, because that was a good word to say in those days.

"By the way," said Keith, "what is that sticking out of your pocket?"

"Nothing. Just something I found," Todd replied as he tucked the rat-tailed bow tie away.

Chapter 3: Ol' Red Gill

The six Bad Guys set out before dawn. After days of planning, they felt confident in their mission, but now it appeared to be easier than they had ever dreamed. A few minutes ago, they stole two boats from a resort, motored upriver, and beached them on the bank below the stand of prickly ash where they now lay hidden. One boat had carried Slip, Slide, and Bruise, while the other hauled Scratch, Cut, and Percy Scarecrow. The way they saw it, there was room for more.

According to their orders, they were to snatch at least one Good Guy from among a group of three or four. While two did the snatching, the other four would hold off the other Good Guys. Now, to their delight, they saw one left alone. When a bunch of crows obliged by setting up a racket, they plowed through the thorny brush, grabbed their quarry, and dragged him to the boats, while the birds' clamor overwhelmed his cries for help. Easy.

They maneuvered the boats upstream past the powerhouse. Here the channel, lacking the water diverted through a canal to run the power plant, grew too narrow, shallow, and rocky to navigate.

Abandoning the first boat and letting it float downstream, they clamored upstream, skipping from rock to rock.

Before releasing the second boat, Percy grabbed a sturdy driftwood limb and punched a hole in its hull, laughing heartily as he did so. Then he tossed several large stones inside to weigh it down. Every few steps he turned around to watch the boats drifting farther down the river. Each time, he saw his boat riding a little lower in the water until, at last, it sank. With every backward glance, he laughed as heartily as the first, and he could scarcely contain his mirth as the craft slipped below the surface.

A short time later, Scratch veered aside onto a fishermen's trail that led up a steep bank. He wrote something on a paper and stuffed it into an envelope, but he did not have it when he returned. "That oughta sour their stew," he said with a sneer.

As Mark, the captured Good Guy, was pulled and shoved along, he was often knocked into the water. Each splash brought with it more wicked laughter, especially when he took a nasty blow on his shin from a submerged rock. "Don't like swimming, Sonnyboy?" roared Percy as he dragged Mark out. Mark turned away and limped on, knowing that a reply would be as futile as trying to fight.

They passed under a busy bridge. Mark hoped that someone crossing it would recognize him in his distress and summon help, but everyone seemed to be too intent on getting their milk to the dairy, their grain to the feed mill, or their letters to the post office. If they noticed the strange band below, they probably passed it off as a group of kids playing. No one gave them a second thought, and no help came.

Upstream from the bridge, a half-mile of pools surrounded by water-worn boulders stretched northwards to the Vermillion Falls dam. Mark thought about the many times he had walked that route for pleasure. Now, when he heard one of his captors mutter to another that they were "making for it," he shivered, not just because he still dripped from his last plunge into the river. No, in his mind he pictured himself being pitched from the dam. The sting of a willow branch whipping across his legs interrupted his thoughts, and he moved forward.

A thousand feet from the dam lay a pool, a hundred or so feet across. A huge finger of solid granite rose like a watchtower on its west side. Between the water and the tower ran a narrow shelf. The Bad Guys formed a single file and edged along it, keeping Mark in the middle. As he reached the thinnest section of ledge, at a point where he had to hug the side of the tower, Mark glanced into the water. His eye caught a glimpse of movement and a flash of red.

In those days, as now, the waters below the dam teemed with fish, most notably rock sturgeons. Some of them had cruised these waters for as many as a hundred years and reached sizes unrivaled by any other creature in the river. One of the oldest and largest was known locally as Ol' Red Gill. Residents had been spotting him for years, and he had become something of a legend in Vermillion Falls. Once, several years earlier, a fisherman from Illinois snagged him near the end of his tail and managed to land him after a great battle. Proudly hauling him to a weigh station in town, he was shocked by the reaction of the townspeople who forced him to return the still-living fish to the river. They also made note, however, that Ol' Red Gill weighed 87 pounds and 9 ounces.

That was years ago, and after recovering from his close call and carrying a scar on his tail as a reminder, Ol' Red Gill prospered and kept on growing. Just then he was drowsing after a mossy meal gleaned from the rocks along the banks of the pool. Now he heard movement on the trail above the surface. He had heard such noises thousands of times before and took little note of it, although he flicked his tail slightly, causing a ripple above.

He was not prepared for what happened next. Nor were the
Bad Guys. With a jab of his forearm, Mark pushed himself away
from the rock and dropped smoothly into the pool. "He's falling in
again," grunted Bruise with a cruel chuckle.

This, however, was no fall. Mark slipped in feet first,
making barely a splash. He turned his body so it hooked
horizontally, right next to Ol' Red Gill whom he clasped in his arms.
The old sturgeon snapped out of his slumber and exploded in a
churning, writhing, twisting burst of energy, like an aquatic Brahma
bull. Mark needed all his strength and determination to hold on, but
somehow he managed to cling firmly to the fish. In an instant, it
reached the middle of the pool and dove, rolling as it went. Mark's
back scraped against a rock. His shoulder slammed into another,
which, fortunately, was loose and rolled aside.

Still Ol' Red Gill flailed about beneath the surface. Mark's
lungs begged for oxygen, but he stubbornly held tight. A moment
later he sensed that the sturgeon was returning to the surface, and he
felt a rush of air around his head. With a gasp, he filled his lungs
and heard himself say, "They are Bad Guys."

Ol' Red Gill's manner changed abruptly. Thrashing no more,
he held close to the surface and swam swiftly to the far side of the

pool where he stopped. Mark loosened his grip and lunged toward a spot where he could clamber out of the water.

Meanwhile, chaos broke out among the Bad Guys. Scratch pushed Cut into the pool, screaming at him to pursue Mark. Bruise jumped up and down on the ledge, shaking his fists and screaming one vile phrase after another. Percy stumbled about, picking up rocks and chunks of driftwood, which he hurled in the general direction of the splashing with little effect (unless you count the stick he bounced off Cut's ear). Slip and Slide, tall, long-legged, and the most sure-footed of the group, kept their heads and lurched off around the pool, one going each way.

Mark knew he had a good start on his captors, but now he struggled. Moss, slime, and water coated the granite, making it difficult to climb ashore. Once he did, he labored to catch his breath. His back and shoulder throbbed from the blows they had taken, and his arms hung at his side, numb from gripping the fish. Slide caught him before he got thirty feet. Slip arrived seconds later, and they hauled him back around the pool, one clutching each arm.

"You'll pay for this," said Slip. Mark was too exhausted to reply or resist.

As they neared the others, Mark saw them glaring at him. "If we didn't have orders from the Old Man, we'd fix you right now, Sonnyboy," screamed Percy.

"Don't think I won't get my satisfaction for this before it's all over," growled Cut as he rubbed his ear. "You'll wish you behaved."

"We'll have our fun yet, and you'll be sorry," said Bruise with another shake of his fist.

Slip and Slide led Mark away toward the dam, but before Bruise and Percy could follow, cold water sprayed against their backs. They turned to see Ol' Red Gill churning up a fountain with his tail.

"Get away from here, ya stinkin' fish," yelled Bruise. "If we had more time, we'd fix you, too."

The sturgeon disappeared under the water, but as the company drew away from the pool, Mark sneaked a peek behind him. He saw a head thrust into the air beside a rock, twenty-some feet out in the pool, and he was certain that an eye followed them.

Soon they reached the dam and found a well-used path leading up the bank on the west side. Climbing it, they came to a road where the Bad Guys stopped to listen. "Car," whispered Slip. They pulled Mark to the ground behind a clump of brush until it passed.

Once satisfied that the road was clear, they crossed it and passed into the woods on the far side. They were now in Bad Guy Country.

Chapter 4: Unexpected Hazards

Bad Guy Country, as the Good Guys call it, is a region covering several hundred square miles. Its southern border lies just north of Keith's family's farm. It is a wild land, heavily forested, dotted with lakes and pockmarked with marshes. It is fit neither for farming nor building for the most part, and so it is sparsely populated, at least by normal people.

In some ways its name is not quite appropriate. While the Bad Guys live there, so do most of the Good Guys. Neither group is particularly anxious to be known to the rest of the world, and this forbidding land provides excellent concealment. The few scrappy farms and homes squeezed into the rare stretches of solid ground are easy to avoid, as are the cabins, cottages, and resorts that cluster around the more accessible lakes. Many of these sit deserted at various times of the year and make attractive targets for Bad Guys' mischief. Were it not for Good Guy protection, few of them would remain.

The woods across from the dam lay near the southeast corner of that region, and once the raiders entered their domain, they made good time hustling Mark off toward their headquarters. Although the path wound its way around swamps, lakes, and impenetrable brush, they knew it well.

The Bad Ghosts lived near this corner. Commonly, various groups of Bad Guys lived in their own colonies and clusters scattered around Bad Guy Country. Sometimes, however, certain members of these groups split off and set up housekeeping wherever pickings seemed fairly easy. In such cases, one could find anywhere from three to ten of them living in some abandoned shack that fit their needs. There they would stay until their little shanty completely fell down. Lifting a finger in the name of upkeep or any other kind of worthwhile cause was virtually unheard of among them. As might be expected, such renegades did not rank among the top troops of the Bad Guys.

Percy Scarecrow *did* live with the Bad Scarecrows and was a fierce fighter, which may have been why he found a place on this day's expedition. The other five belonged to a group known as Unexpected Hazards' Henchmen, his most trusted followers. They lived around Bad Guy headquarters and knew all the shortcuts to it.

They brought Mark in early that afternoon and found the main hall nearly deserted. A musty odor made Mark wrinkle his nose. At a table in a corner sat a hulking figure and a sinister fellow with horns growing from above his ears. They clutched playing cards in their hands.

Mark recognized them: Clumsy Giant and Drunken Devil. Abandoned shack residents, they often hung around headquarters in hopes of getting a free meal. Now they were deep in thought, concentrating on their game. Clumsy stared long and hard at his cards. He scowled. He wrinkled his brow. He squinted his eyes and scratched his head. At length, he said, "Go fish."

Scratch interrupted the game. "We need you to help Percy guard the prisoners while we go find the Old Man."

Percy Scarecrow's eyes flashed. "Hold on there a minute, Sonnyboy. I'm not letting you five go to the Old Man and take all the credit. Next you'll bring him in here so it looks like I'm hanging around with these guys." He jerked his thumb in the direction of the card players. "Oh, no! I'm getting my piece of this pie."

"Did you say pie?" said Clumsy, licking his lips.

"Fear not, my old pal," said Scratch to Percy. "We promise to cut you in on this."

"Cut me a piece, too," said Clumsy.

Percy ignored Clumsy and turned to Scratch. "Oh sure, just like you were going to cut me in on that wedding cake you stole last week. Uh, uh. I'm going along, Sonnyboy. These two can watch the brat for that long."

Five more minutes of squabbling produced a decision. Mark would be locked in a closet while Clumsy and Drunken sat on chairs directly outside it. Percy, still angry, would accompany the others as they sought "the Old Man." Thus, the six captors left, growling dire warnings about keeping a close eye on Mark and to not let him out.

A short time later, the guards heard a knock at the closet door. "Shut up, kid. We ain't leavin' you out," said Clumsy.

"I don't want out. I just want to show you something."

"Forget it, kid," said Drunken. "We don't want to see your ugly face. Haw, haw, haw."

"It's not that. It's something you'll like."

Drunken Devil rubbed his chin. "What do you think, Clumsy? Should we take a look?"

"I don't know. They told us not to let him out."

"But we wouldn't be letting him out, just looking at what he has to show us. They did tell us to keep an eye on him. Pretty hard when he's behind a door. Maybe it's something we can take and use. Or maybe it's something we can give the Old Man and get a big reward."

"I don't know. What if we got in trouble, Drunken?"

"What kind of trouble could we get in? There's two of us, and we're both bigger'n him. Especially you."

"Are you two going to open the door, or am I going to show this to the Old Man myself?" said Mark.

Drunken Devil could contain himself no longer. He stood up, stepped to the door, opened it, and stood wide-eyed in wonder. Mark was holding out a penny. "Money!" cried Drunken, pronouncing the ey as a short i. "Money!" he repeated. "Money to buy…whiskey, rah, ha, ha!"

In an instant, Clumsy stood beside him, staring greedily, his elbow ready to shove his partner aside. They hesitated for a split-second, just long enough for Mark to roll the penny along the floor between them. Turning their heads down and in to watch it make a slow, graceful arc into a corner, they bumped them together. The bump jolted them from their reverie, and they bolted for the corner in a wild scramble for the coin.

Mark, meanwhile, scrambled for the door. Passing through, he dashed into a hallway and turned left. All doors in that direction were locked. He whirled and sped to the other end. As he flashed past the hallway door, Clumsy Giant spotted him and remembered his orders. "You tricked us," he bellowed as he stumbled toward the hall.

"Let's get him," shouted Drunken Devil rising to follow, but not before he pocketed the penny.

Had he been outside, Mark could have outrun both of them easily, but in an unfamiliar building, he was trapped and confused. Finding an open side room, he tipped over a chair to block the entrance, gaining valuable seconds as Clumsy fell face first over it, kicking Drunken in the shin as he sprawled to the floor. With the two Bad Guys angrily howling at each other, Mark had a chance to look around. He saw what appeared to be a door leading outside and left partly ajar. He lunged toward it.

Clumsy cried, "Stop him before the Old Man finds out," but Mark's hand already gripped the knob. A second later, with a glance back at his pursuers, he felt a rush of fresh air. As he turned back to get his bearings, a blow to his forehead drove him back and slammed him against the outer wall. A black clad figure grabbed him and threw him back through the door and onto the floor.

Clumsy and Drunken stood frozen, their mouths hanging open and the color draining from their faces. The dark figure glared at them and then at Mark before declaring what Mark already knew: "I'm Unexpected Hazards."

Chapter 5: Into Bad Guy Country

Keith and Todd bustled about, gathering gear for their "camping trip." They packed knapsacks with extra clothes for themselves and Rick. Keith told Todd that he would pack for Mark, and he put a couple of Mark's things on top of his own for show. While Todd rolled four sleeping bags, Keith went to the garage and hid the fishing equipment that Rick had supposedly already taken. He put new batteries in a large flashlight and brought a small cooking kit from the kitchen. At last they gathered everything together next to Todd's bed.

"How can we carry all this? Why don't Rick and Mark come and help?" asked Todd.

"We can handle it. We'll make them carry most of it on the way back. I'll take anything you can't. Why don't you haul some of it down to the porch?"

Todd picked up his knapsack, a sleeping bag, and the flashlight. "Uh, wait a minute with that," Keith said, pointing at the flashlight. "It's not ready yet."

"But you just put batteries in it."

41

"I need to check the bulb. Here." He handed Todd the cooking kit. "I'll be right down." When Todd left, Keith climbed onto the bed and held the flashlight up to the light fixture. A small figure climbed out of the latter and into the former.

In the end, they did carry all that and more. Their mothers and grandmother insisted upon sending several pounds of food with them. "You boys are foolish if you think you can survive on fish and berries," said Grandma. Along with the food came warnings to be careful and not do anything dangerous.

"Don't worry," said Todd, but Keith remained silent. He reached down and squeezed the green, berry-shaped blossom of a plant growing along the edge of the driveway, one they called pineapple weed, and offered another to Todd. The sweet smell its blossom left on his fingers recalled memories of good times in Junes past.

"Don't you love that smell?" Keith asked.

He hoisted his burden onto his back and helped Todd with his load. "See you in a few days," he called back as they started down the driveway to the barn and beyond. "I hope," he mumbled to himself.

###

The sun's last rays were slipping from Buckwheat Hill as they approached it. Todd's shoulders already ached, and Keith was more than ready to put down his pack. For the last hundred feet or so, a noise (or was it just something stirring in the back of his head?) had been gradually growing in Todd's ears. Now his head snapped up, and his ears strained. Rounding the south end of the hill, the flat part of the field came into view. Todd saw that it was covered with Good Guys, hundreds of them. Rick, the Lugu, and Marc Monster ran down from the hilltop to greet the two.

Todd looked at them, his head tilted at a strange angle. He looked up the hill. He looked at the flat. "Where's Mark?"

No one answered for several seconds. Marc Monster and the Lugu stared at the ground and kicked at the dirt. Finally, Rick said, "We don't know."

"What do you mean?"

"We don't know," Rick repeated and paused before continuing, "because the Bad Guys have him."

Todd turned to Keith and back to Rick. "You're fooling me. It's not a good joke, Rick."

Rick just shook his head and said, "That's why everyone is here, and you're not supposed to be. You're the last ones to arrive. I'm sorry. I have to talk to everyone now." He turned and walked partway up the hill. Todd followed, looking wildly this way and that. He was supposed to be going camping with Mark. This could not be!

Rick waved to the crowd, and the field fell silent. "By now I'm sure you all know why you were called here," he began in his most formal speech-voice. "This morning, Keith and I made a mistake, a careless mistake that has cost us dearly. We left Mark alone not far from here, and now the Bad Guys have him."

A low murmur rose and gradually died down.

"Now we've gathered you together to end all the rumors and to warn you of the danger we face at this time. With the success they had in capturing him, we're concerned that they may be encouraged to do more, possibly by attempting to kidnap others in our leadership group. Our scouts will be doubly alert, but we ask you all to take care. Don't venture out except in groups.

"We have no plan yet. In fact, we may never have one. All I can say now is that Keith and I will go into hiding." He frowned and looked at Keith. "And Todd as well, it seems. It may be the only way to keep us safe."

Another murmur rippled across the field. Cries of "No!" and "Never!" rang out from the crowd.

Todd's eyes widened, and his mouth opened, aghast. He whispered to Keith, "That's not right. Rick would never do that." But Keith just motioned to him to be quiet.

When silence returned to the field, Rick resumed. "We also have information telling us that great harm will come to Mark if we interfere with the Bad Guys' actions. Therefore, I must ask you to do as I say. Our day as protector of this region may be over."

The murmur rose again, stronger than before. Todd wanted to scream, but all that came from his mouth was a whispered, "No-o-o-o."

Rick raised his hand. "Before you leave, I want a leader from each group to meet with us on top of Buckwheat Hill. They'll advise you of your next step. For now I ask you to take care of yourselves and your friends. Maybe somehow someone will come up with a solution to all this, but I have little hope right now. I'm sorry."

Rick hung his head and turned, dragging himself slowly up the hill. No ripple followed, only a stunned hush, a disbelieving hush, a defeated hush. Tears poured down Todd's cheeks and dampened his shirt. Keith helped him to his feet and, without a word, led him after Rick. They had nearly reached the summit when

Satch Scarecrow jogged up to them from the side. Todd heard Keith whisper to him, "Did they hear it?"

Satch nodded. "At least one, possibly two confirmed." Keith gave him a thumbs-up signal and hurried to join Rick.

Once they and the other leaders reached the hilltop, Rick gathered them into a tight huddle. "I have to say that I'm sorry one more time," he said in a low tone. "We *do* have a plan, and we are *not* giving up. I said what I said for a purpose. We wanted the Bad Guys to hear my speech. We want them to believe we are capitulating."

"That means giving up," Keith whispered to Todd.

"Do we know if they overheard?" Rick asked Keith. Keith pointed at Satch.

"Our scouts spotted two of theirs in the woods below the field," said Satch. "Yes, they overheard."

"I also wanted an honest reaction from our people," Rick continued. "Some of you know our plan already. I don't want to say too much right now, but don't worry that we are not going to just 'hole up' somewhere. You can tell your groups when you get home. Just be sure no one is eavesdropping. And stay alert. We may need you at any time.

"As for us, we need to be on our way. Marc Monster will accompany us, and our scouts are watching our route, so we should be safe for the time being. Take care, my friends."

The gathering broke up. Rick, Keith, Todd, and Marc Monster bundled their gear together. The pile looked smaller than before—the Lugu had already left with a knapsack and two sleeping bags—and with two extra carriers, Todd was relieved to bear a much lighter load. He was even more relieved to hear the latest news.

The foursome left the field and set out to the north along a narrow, well-worn cow path that ran between the crick and the field. The path rose gradually, made a slight bend around a gigantic oak tree, and descended again. A short distance later, Todd heard a sound like someone plucking a single note on a one-string banjo. He looked in the general direction of the crick but saw nothing. "What was that?" he asked.

"A bullfrog," Keith replied. "I always seem to hear it in this same spot. Every time I go past here to get the cows or to bring them home it croaks like that. Just once whenever we pass. It gets so I barely notice it, but I probably would if I didn't hear it."

Soon the stars began to peek out, one by one, through the breaks in the trees. At the same time, earthbound stars, the fireflies, appeared. At first the walkers saw individuals flickering as they meandered above the pasture. As the warm June night darkened, a whole galaxy of them flashed and sparkled, some white and some almost green, silent fireworks anticipating Independence Day to come.

Unfortunately, the fireflies were not the only insects in the evening sky. Todd became aware of a low humming sound that slowly grew in intensity. Rick slapped at his leg. "It's a good thing I brought this," Keith said, pulling a can of mosquito repellant from his pack. "This is about as safe as we are going to be in terms of Bad Guys, so I don't want these skeeters to ruin things."

Watching them spray each other down, Marc Monster laughed and mumbled something about those "thin skinned humans."

When they had marched almost a half-mile upstream, they reached a point where the two branches of the crick joined each other. Keith led them along the right hand tributary, saying it would be easier to follow at night. Crossing over two barbwire fences and a road running between them, they reached a cornfield where the young sprouts grew barely four inches high. The glow of a moon just approaching its fullness gave them the light they needed to follow carefully between the rows. "Our neighbor wouldn't appreciate us trampling it," said Keith.

The night breeze carried the scent of new mown hay to them, and Todd breathed in the sweet smell. A sound like the clatter of wooden wind chimes made him jump. "Sandhill cranes," said Keith.

The field ended, and they were forced to cross three more fences, one separating the field from a narrow stretch of pastureland, and two more on either side of a gravel road. Night now ruled the sky, but a greater darkness loomed beyond that last fence. A thick forest towered before them, the boundary of Bad Guy Country.

"I hate to call attention to ourselves, but we'll need the flashlight now," said Rick.

Keith dug it out of a backpack, but as he did he fumbled it, and it fell to the ground. "Ouch!" it seemed to say in a squeaky voice.

"Sorry," said Keith.

"George!" said Todd. "Is he coming, too?"

"Either that or we have a talking flashlight," said Rick.

Todd smiled. "Neat."

At first the forest seemed like an inviting place. At their feet the light shone on clusters of wild strawberries. The neighbor's cows had kept the grass short and free from briars. As the trees grew thicker, patches of blackcap and raspberry bushes promised a sweet delight in the coming weeks. Before long the trees grew tall and thick, drowning out most of the underbrush. The travelers stepped easily through this section until they reached still another fence.

"This is the end of our neighbor's farm," Keith whispered. "I don't know who owns the land beyond, if anyone."

Now the forest changed abruptly. Downed trees lay scattered and tangled everywhere, and the brush thickened. Here and there, large patches of thorn apples and prickly ash forced them to change their route, as did frequent marshes. The darkness made it difficult to travel through this section of woods, and everyone agreed that they would be in trouble without the flashlight.

Just past one great tangle of thorns and burrs they entered a clearing. The light shown on a trash heap filled with litter, bones, burnt out stumps, and filth of every description. The bark had been hacked from the trunks of several unlucky, still-standing trees. Some had scrawled curses and threats carved into them. Many were covered with common vulgarities and others with phrases like, "SKIN YA ALIV AN DRINK YER BLUD."

"Typical Bad Guys stuff," said Marc Monster.

"Sick," thought Todd.

They continued northward, jogging to the east or west as obstacles blocked their path. Along the way they spotted more signs of Bad Guys. Todd imagined them cursing and cackling as they vented their malice on the forest. He shuddered to think that his brother was in such hands.

He hardly noticed as the disgusting signs dwindled. Suddenly the woods opened up, and a small house appeared, light shining from its windows. He jumped behind the nearest tree and felt his heart beating furiously.

"What are you doing?" Rick asked, right out loud.

"Is that a Bad Guy house?"

"Take a look," said Marc Monster. "Can you imagine them keeping a place this neat? This is our place."

The front door opened, and the Lugu stepped out. "How ya doin', folks?" he said.

Chapter 6: A Proper Punishment

Unexpected Hazards stood over Mark, one hand on his hip and the other stroking his black handlebar mustache, as if daring him to try to get away. Mark knew better. He looked up at the leader of the Bad Guys and saw a figure that many people might find vaguely familiar.

He was old, older than anyone alive, but he looked like a man in his early middle years. Common wisdom among the Good Guys said that his longevity stemmed from some unholy deal made in the remote past. Indeed, his image was well known more than a hundred years ago. Whether he had appeared more openly then or because the very rumor of him had crept into people's foulest nightmares, he became the model for the villain in the melodramas of that time.

He dressed his bony body in black, from his boots to his top hat. A cape hung from his neck, and he would wrap himself in it even on the hottest days. It seemed, in fact, that he felt no earthly heat or cold. Perhaps his depth of wickedness insulated him from all that. His mustache perched between a sharp nose and a mouth prone to sneering and showing sharp, white teeth, an uncommon color among the yellows and greens of most Bad Guys. His chin jutted out nearly as sharply as his nose. Beneath his top hat hung straight, jet-black hair that shone with enough grease to make it immobile in all but the fiercest wind.

When he spoke, Mark noticed the sharpest feature of all, a voice that rasped like a buzz saw. When he barked, even his followers cringed in fear of the keen edge of that voice. Whether Mark saw it or not, they were cringing now. Behind Unexpected Hazards, Mark's six captors backed away slowly. Unexpected jerked his hand from his handlebar and pointed a long finger behind him, waggling it back and forth.

"You six don't think you are going anywhere, do you?" he asked without looking at them. They looked at each other, however, and stopped in their tracks. His eyes flashed at Drunken Devil and Clumsy Giant. "Were you two supposed to be watching him?"

Drunken tried to look dumb, a task as easy for him as it was for Clumsy. Clumsy shrugged and mumbled, "Reckon so."

"Reckon so!" barked Unexpected. "Reckon so. So what was he doing outside the door? Playing hide and seek?"

He turned to the other six. "Who put these idiots in charge?"

Slip pointed at Percy. "We told him to stay here, but he just had to come with us to find you."

Percy shouted back, "Like I'm going to let you get all the credit, Sonnyboy. Any one of these precious henchmen could have stayed and guarded him, but no. They're all too high and mighty. Let Percy do all the dirty work while…."

"Don't worry," said Unexpected. "You will all get full credit--full credit for almost botching the job and letting the prisoner escape."

"But, Boss," Bruise pleaded. "We done what you said. We caught the little vermin and brung him here. It weren't our fault that them two clowns couldn't keep an eye on him."

"No, but it was your fault that they got the chance to do it. I won't put up with this incompetence. You are all going to get the Proper punishment for this."

Mark saw desperation on the faces of his captors. They began pointing at each other, making accusations. Unexpected stood, unhearing and unyielding. At last he hissed one word, "Silence." As if someone had thrown a switch, the room went still. "Now, on to the meeting room," he continued. "Bring the prisoner along if you think you can get him that far without losing him."

Scratch and Cut each grasped one of Mark's arms and led him along behind Unexpected. The forlorn group marched silently down the hall until they came to a closed door. Mark recognized it as one he had tried to open, only to find it locked. Unexpected unlocked it and motioned for the group to enter. "Sit down," he said. Then he left the room.

The muttering resumed immediately.

"It was your fault."

"We wouldn't have caught him without me."

"You were just trying to butter up to the Old Man."

"We would've caught him."

"You never listen to orders."

"You idiots cost us a reward."

On and on it went. In the midst of it, Slide pointed at Mark. "It was his fault."

At this, the wrath of the whole group redirected itself at Mark. They rose and moved toward him, cursing with every step. Mark braced himself, but at that moment Unexpected Hazards returned, and everyone sat down with a hush. Mark sensed a great dread settling over them as they waited unmoving and unspeaking for the next five minutes.

A lone chair stood at the front of the room. All the Bad Guys stared at it. Clumsy wiped sweat from his forehead, elbowing Cut's head in the process. Mark expected a quarrel, but Cut's attention remained glued to the chair. At length, a side door opened, and a skeleton stepped inside, carrying a book. It strutted to the chair, sat down, crossed its legs, and opened the book.

Proper Skeleton was much despised among the other Bad Guys. He had a terribly misplaced arrogance, thinking of himself as an intellectual, aristocratic, and refined. Neither a strong fighter nor a great creator of mischief, he preferred the "thinking skeleton's" life. The pride of his life was his book, *Poems for the Pompous*, a rewrite of nursery rhymes and other common verse done in his own style. In this, Unexpected Hazards found him useful.

With a haughty look at the group, Proper cleared his throat, an act Mark thought quite peculiar for a skeleton. Then he began reading.

> "A triumvirate of visually impaired rodents,
>
> A triumvirate of visually impaired rodents,
>
> Observe their mode of perambulation.
>
> Observe their mode of perambulation.
>
> In toto, they pursued the spouse of an agrarian
>
> individual
>
> Who detached their posterior appendages with a keen
>
> implement of cutlery.
>
> Have you, in the course of your existence, observed
>
> as singular a phenomenon

As a triumvirate of visually impaired rodents?"

As he read, Mark saw the Bad Guys grimacing as if they had just eaten a skunk sandwich and squirming like worms covered with itching powder. Some tried to plug their ears, but as soon as one's hands reached his ear, a look from Unexpected made him drop them back to his sides. Proper droned on through several more poems.

As Mark watched his captors react, he smiled for the first time that day.

Chapter 7: A Journey Out of Time

Todd awoke with a start. A fly had been buzzing around his head for some time, and he had been swiping at it in his sleep. When it landed on his nose, his eyes popped open. The ceiling in his room at his grandparents' never looked like this. Quickly sitting up, his gaze panned across an unfamiliar setting. Then he saw Rick and Keith talking softly in a corner, and he remembered.

Rick heard him stirring and turned to him. "It's about time you woke up. We were just about to roust you our own way. It's time for breakfast."

Todd yawned. This house belonged to the Lugu, his cousins the Gugu and the Cuckoo, and Marc Monster. He felt safe in it. Rolling over to a spot where a ray of sunlight struck the bed, he stretched. He felt a warm and pleasant breeze and saw it gently ruffling the curtains. The temptation to lie back and enjoy the comfort of the moment lost out to two things: Rick and Keith shaking the bed and the smell of bacon and eggs cooking.

Todd pulled on his clothes, and a minute later all three marched into the kitchen where they found the Lugu and Gugu bustling about in polka-dotted aprons. Todd laughed to himself at the sight. The Lugu stood, spatula in hand, tending the bacon. The Gugu, shorter, squatter, and rounder of face, washed and cut up fruit.

"How ya doin', folks?" said the Lugu with a cheery grin. "Are you ready to eat? The Cuckoo is setting the table. You can go in and have a glass of milk or wild grape juice."

"Do you have any Sugar Honey Crunchies?" asked Todd.

The Lugu and Gugu looked at each other curiously. Rick kicked Todd lightly on the side of his leg and made a back and forth motion with his hand that told him to ask no more such questions.

"Just kidding," said Todd. "I'm starved."

"Well, that's right good," said the Gugu. "We don't know much about them crunchy thangs, but we're fixin' a right tasty meal for y'all. Reckon you'll be needin' some nourishment. Sounds like y'all got a right hefty hike ahead o' you."

Todd shot a puzzled look at Rick and Keith, but they were already heading into the dining room. The Cuckoo greeted and seated them. His tall, thin body looked gangly and awkward to Todd, but he moved with a grace and ease that proved otherwise. He vanished into the kitchen and returned with a pitcher of milk and another of a sparkling, purple juice. He filled their cups quickly and deftly, without spilling a drop.

"Where's Marc Monster?" asked Todd.

"He's packing. He's going with you, you know," said the Cuckoo.

"Marc's coming? Neat!"

"Me, too," said the Lugu, who had just entered carrying a platter of bacon and eggs.

"Double neat," said Todd. Before he could say more, the Gugu and Marc Monster joined them. They sat down to a huge meal that included wild strawberries, rough grained bread (some toasted in honor of the guests' preferences), and butter to go with the main fare.

Everyone dug in heartily except for Todd who picked at a few items. (He really would have preferred the Crunchies.) Rick looked at him, finished a mouthful, and whispered, "Todd, you need to eat. The Gugu is right about the big hike."

"Where *are* we going?" Todd asked.

"Tonight," said Rick, "We should be eating supper with the good dinosaurs."

Breakfast done, they strapped on their gear. Rick loaded George back into the flashlight after he had spent a night in the house lights. "It does get a bit cramped in here," the little fellow said as he entered the flashlight.

They stepped out into a meadow where two cows contentedly munched on grass. "Just enough to keep us in milk, butter, and cheese," the Gugu said. A small flock of chickens scratched around the edge of the taller grass. "Just enough to keep us in eggs."

The sun's rays beat upon them as they crossed the meadow. A trickle of sweat crept down Keith's backbone. Rick fanned himself with the cap he had been wearing. They were glad they would be spending most of the day in the cool shade of the woods. Reaching the edge of the meadow, they gave goodbye handshakes to the Gugu and Cuckoo, who wished them a safe trip. With a final wave, they turned and disappeared into the vast, green expanse that is northern Wisconsin in summer.

As the morning wore on, fluffy clouds drifted across the once-clear sky like cattle grazing in a wide, blue pasture. Rick, Keith, and Todd took off their shirts after applying a good dose of mosquito repellent. Todd could hardly believe the numbers of these annoying creatures buzzing around him, especially during mid-day. He was further disgusted by the appearance of a flight of dragonflies. He swatted at one, but Keith stopped him.

"They eat mosquitoes," Keith said. Suddenly, Todd felt a great affection for them.

Before long, Todd saw the marshes closing in on both sides. "Are we going to have to wade through these things?" he asked.

"No," said Marc Monster. "We are coming to a creek, and this is one of the few places we can get to a crossing without having to slog through the muck." He went on to describe the makeup of the area and how he had planned a route through it.

That reminded the Lugu of a comic song about swamps. He began in a low voice.

> "If you like quicksand, snakes, and frogs,
> And hearing gators chomp,
> Mosquito bites, and slimy logs,
> Then come down to the swamp.
>
> A frog sat on a lily pad
> And ate a tasty fly.
> And for dessert that night he had
> A leech and grubworm pie."

Marc Monster, Keith, and Rick joined in on the chorus.

> "If you like quicksand, snakes, and frogs,
> And hearing gators chomp,

Mosquito bites, and slimy logs,
Then come down to the swamp."

Marc Monster chimed in with a verse.

"The Skillery Skallery Alligate
Swum up and bit my toe.

I whacked him on his domed pate.
A lump began to grow."

Everyone now joined in the chorus, even George whose shrill voice
provided an inharmonious counterpoint to the others'. The land rose
up toward the crest of a small ridge, and their voices rose with it. So
it was that they did not hear the chopping and hacking until they
reached the hilltop.

"If you like quicksand, snakes, and frogs,
And hearing gators chomp,
Mosquito bites, and slimy..."

Rick's hand snapped up in warning, and the song ended
abruptly. Below them three goblins were busily mutilating a tree.
The Good Guys slowly backed away, but before they could conceal

themselves behind the hill, one of the goblins looked up and saw Keith.

"Ho, boys, we've got company. Maybe we should go give him a nice welcome," the goblin said. The others grinned and started up the hill until they saw that Keith was not alone. As quickly as they had advanced, they whirled and dashed into the forest.

Rick, Marc Monster, the Lugu, and Todd took a few steps toward the retreating Bad Guys before Keith stopped them. "We'll never catch them. By the time we reached the woods, the only way to follow would be by tracking. That takes time, and you never know what we might run into in the meantime. Our goal is to reach the dinosaurs'. If those goblins run home and spread the word that we're headed there, so much the better."

"You're right," said Rick. "We need to be more careful from now on, though."

Their trail again descended until they heard the creek gurgling ahead. Passing through a short stretch of trees, they reached a steep bank, its edge covered with ferns. At the bottom, the creek bubbled through a tumble of rocks with solid ground on both sides before flowing into a large marshy area. Finding a route where the gaps between stones allowed them to skip from one to the other, they gained the far side.

A harsh voice called out. "What'sa matter, ya' chicken-livered Good Guys?" it said. "Afraid to come down and fight us?"

Across the marsh below, the three goblins stood mocking them. "That's why you ran away into the forest, I suppose," answered Marc Monster.

"We were just getting set up. We would've fixed you good."

"That's easy for you to say from across that swamp where we can't reach you," said the Lugu.

The goblin jeered. "Well, you brave gentlemen can be big heroes when there are only three of us and five of you."

"Six," squeaked George from within the flashlight.

Rick shouted, "Three or thirty, no matter. We'd still whip you."

"Good Guy," the goblin yelled with a scowl and a shake of the fist, "I hate you!" He spat out the word "hate." "You know that?"

"Oh, no," Rick called back. "I thought you loved me."

Completely missing the sarcasm in Rick's voice, the goblins howled with laughter. The leader went on. "Well, we don't. Everybody hates you, you swine. And we'll teach you a lesson if

you try coming around here again." He turned to his buddies.
"C'mon boys, we've got better things to do." With a shake of their
backsides in the direction of Rick, they sauntered into the woods,
jeering and catcalling as they went.

"What a bunch of fools," said Todd.

Marc monster shook his head, "The more you're around Bad
Guys, the more you realize they have their own way of thinking...or
not thinking. They understand what they want to, even if it is not
what is meant."

"One thing they do understand," said Keith, "is that we are a
small group traveling through isolated country, their country. I think
we'd best get moving if we are going to reach the dinosaurs' lake."

From then on they hurried through the woods, trying to make
as little noise as possible. Hunger gnawed at Todd, and he wished he
had taken Rick's advice about breakfast. There would be no time for
lunch. At the same time, the mosquito repellent started to wear off.
Rick, Keith, and Todd did their best to slap silently, but at last they
had to stop to apply more. Also, although the shade of the forest
helped, the heat sapped their energy, and their shirts, put back on to
help stop the mosquitoes, hung limp and damp on their backs.

They reached a thick section of woods where the sunlight
struggled to get through. Keith's watch said five o'clock, but he

might have guessed that evening was coming on. Their pace slowed. Suddenly, Marc Monster stopped and stood on his toes. He tilted his head to one side.

"What's up?" whispered Keith.

"Nothing, maybe, but I'm going to drop back and check something out. Keep moving."

They continued on cautiously for a few hundred feet before they heard Marc Monster crashing through the brush behind them. "Don't worry about making noise," he shouted. "There are about fifty goblins and skeletons hot on our trail."

Todd broke into a dead run, but Rick grabbed his arm. "We'll do best to jog. If we sprint, we'll just wear ourselves out."

In that thick forest, even jogging wore them out quickly. Branches whipped across their faces. Thorny brush grabbed at their pant legs and scratched their arms. Hidden roots tripped more than one of them. They had endured more than twenty minutes of this when they noticed light shining ahead of them.

Voices drifted through the trees behind them. The light grew. Just as they started making out individual cursing and cackling from their pursuers, they burst out into a wide path. They looked to the right and left. The voices got closer.

"This way, folks," the Lugu shouted. "This is the dinosaurs'
path."

New hope arose in Todd, but the others knew that they had
over a mile to go to the lake where the dinosaurs lived. Cresting a
hill, Keith looked back to see the first pair of Bad Guys tumble out
onto the path. He heard them scream something about cutting them
off and saw them pointing for others to angle through the woods.
Moments later, the Bad Guys had all reached the trail. The closest
were only two or three hundred feet behind them. Some brandished
swords, and others carried spears. They would soon be close enough
to hurl them.

"We need to sprint for it now," Keith yelled.

Rick led the race down the hill and had just rounded a bend
when his heart sank. Someone lurked in the trees beside the path
ahead. With no time to weigh the options, he decided that their only
hope was to charge through the ambushers. Barely missing a step,
he roared, "Attack!" and dashed forward.

A second later, he laughed. Stepping from the forest and
standing fast before him was not a band of the enemy, but rather the
good dinosaurs. He and the rest of the group flew into their midst in
one instant. In another, the first two Bad Guys rounded the corner
and were struck down on the spot by the sweep of a stegosaurus' tail.

In a third, the rest of them whirled and scampered back up the path in a great tumult.

Out of breath, Todd collapsed in a patch of soft grass, safe and secure. Surrounded by the dinosaurs, he felt like he had stepped back millions of years in time. But then he realized what time it really was—suppertime.

Chapter 8: The Hidden Haven

The Good Dinosaurs live in a small colony beside a remote lake. Although it may appear on human maps under some human name, the dinosaurs call it Blue Lake, and so shall we.

Five families make up the bulk (in more ways than one) of the population: the Brontosauruses, the Plateosauruses, the Stegosauruses, the Triceratopses, and the Tyrannosauruses. Before anyone becomes alarmed at the close proximity of the first four families with the last, a few facts may be in order.

Eons ago the ancestors of the Tyrannosauruses were the most fearsome predators ever to walk the earth, much as countless books and movies portray them to this day. There came a time, however, when the world changed, and all who did not change with it disappeared forever. Tyrannosaurus Rex needed to change more than most, but few did. Those few started the line of the Blue Lake family. Living peacefully with their neighbors, they learned to survive on a diet of fish, amply provided by the lake, and vegetation that they have come to enjoy.

The other families share similar histories. The mild-mannered Plateosauruses, much smaller than the Tyrannosauruses, also walk on two legs and are the only other family that eats fish as well as plants. Much admired for their speed and agility, they are ever ready to run errands for their neighbors. They tend to be shy and quiet, but the others hold them in high respect.

The gargantuan Brontosauruses spend a great deal of time in the lake, their long necks craned above the surface as they enjoy the water on a sunny day. They have always preferred aquatic plants for their diets but will easily accept leaves, grasses, fruits, or vegetables. They love to eat and are constantly developing new and delicious recipes for everything from pond algae to rutabagas. In recent years, science has renamed their species "Apatosaurus," but they have held to their former name. "It's a grand old name and part of our heritage," says Mr. Brontosaurus.

The Stegosauruses prefer to stay on dry land and to eat the plants they find there. Although relatively slow moving, they have incredible strength and endurance. The bony plates on their backs help protect them from attack, but they also serve to collect the sun's energy when fanned out. They have been known to jokingly refer to themselves as the "solar-powered dinosaurs."

The Triceratopses, with three horns on their faces and a shield around their necks, look fierce from the front but are peaceful and good-natured unless threatened. They share the Stegosauruses' eating habits. They are some of the quickest dinosaurs, both in movement and in wit, and they are generally at the center of the organization of any special events in the lake colony.

Having lived together for so long, they tend to use nicknames for each other. Thus, they call each other the Brontos, the Plates, the Tys, the Stegs, and the Tris.

In addition to the five families, the Blue Lake colony boasts four other residents. In a pair of caves in a nearby hill, live two cavemen. Their original names, Og and Ak, have long since been forgotten. One of them serves as the medicine man for the colony and as its leader among the Good Guys. Baby dinosaurs (and dinosaurs consider their young to be babies, not even naming them until they are quite well grown) love to visit him because he always has a story to tell. They know him as Friendly Doctor.

Friendly Doctor employs an assistant, a red, two-legged dinosaur with a duck like bill and a single hornlike projection thrust from the back of his head. A flap of skin, much like the webbing of a duck's feet, stretches from the horn to the back of his neck. (Scientists would call him a parasaurolophus.) He does many odd jobs for Friendly Doctor and anyone else who needs a hand, and so he is called Jack, short for Jack-of-all-trades.

Everyone calls the other caveman Family Paper Boy because he keeps them current on all the news of the area and anything involving Good Guy business. A green pteronodon, a great winged dinosaur, assists him in gathering the news. His flying ability is often invaluable to the dinosaurs. He also serves as an unofficial alarm clock due to his habit of waking with the sun and taking a flight around the lake for a morning stretch, cawing like a crow as he flies. Because of this, they call him Family Rooster.

So they pass the years, living in peace with each other and with malice towards none. None, that is, except for another colony of far less respectable cavemen and dinosaurs that have plagued them since beyond memory. Long ago, this group aligned itself with the Bad Guys. Soon after that, the Blue Lake dinosaurs found the Good Guys and have been members ever since.

Once the dinosaurs repelled the attack, they waited a few minutes for the travelers, exhausted and drenched with sweat, to catch their breath. Numerous long, and sometimes deep, scratches striped the new arrivals' bodies, and mosquito bites dotted them, itching terribly. Even George needed a break. The jostling he took as they ran with the flashlight had left him shaken.

"We can make you feel a lot better when we get you back to the lake," said Friendly Doctor.

Moving slowly, they set off on the last mile of their journey. At first, Todd doubted that he could make it, but with each step he found enough strength for one more. His body ached, and his stomach growled.

At last they reached Blue Lake. Todd looked all around, a puzzled expression on his face. Expecting to see a small village (although with very large houses), he saw no houses at all. Here and there a mound rose up, and he thought he saw a cave entrance in the hill, but he was not sure. "Is this the right lake?" he asked.

"It is if you are looking for us," said Mr. Tri. He smiled at Todd. "Those mounds you see are our homes. You know we don't want to be obvious, so we try to make things blend in with the landscape."

Mr. Bronto led them to a large knoll near the lake. He pulled a root sticking out of a steep bank. Todd had seen no signs of a door, but now the bank opened, and they entered a hallway the size of a barn. Mrs. Bronto poked her long neck out of a side door and welcomed her guests. Below her, a smaller neck peeked out and shyly ducked back inside.

"Supper is almost ready," she said. "Find yourselves a seat at the small table in the dining room."

"They will be ready in a few minutes, dear," said Mr. Bronto. "I'll take them to get cleaned up first. Then Friendly Doctor has some work to do on them."

He led them to a room where a spring bubbled from a fissure in the wall and trickled along a chiseled course before channeling into a number of pools. The travelers eagerly splashed the sweat from their bodies and relaxed in the coolness. By the time they dried themselves, Friendly Doctor arrived. He spread a white salve on their scratches and a green one on the mosquito bites. Their bodies felt immediate soothed, and they thanked him profusely.

Mr. Bronto led them to the dining room. Upon a large table (for the Brontos) and a small table (for everyone else) was set a supper of wild rice in a sauce made with tomatoes, onions, celery, and a variety of wild herbs. A dessert, with a main ingredient that seemed to be wild berries, followed. This time Todd did no picking. Mrs. Bronto laughed when he said he had never eaten so much. At the main table, a young brontosaurus watched Todd as he ate, but whenever Todd looked at him, he lowered his eyes.

After supper, they joined the rest of the colony in the village hall, a gigantic room built into the side of the hill near Friendly

Doctor's cave. The caveman made a few introductory remarks and called Rick and Keith to the front.

"The time has come to reveal our plan," said Rick, reverting to his speaking voice. "We've come here to lull the Bad Guys into thinking we are obeying their commands and are hiding out for our own safety. Actually, we will be leaving shortly after dark through the Brontos' runway to the lake. Keith, Marc Monster, the Lugu, George, and I will then make our way (in secret, we hope) to Bad Guy headquarters."

Todd's eyes, which had been drooping, opened wide, and his mouth dropped open. He drew his hands to his chest, pointing at himself with all his fingers as he silently mouthed the words, "And me?"

Rick pretended not to see. "We hope that Family Rooster can fly reconnaissance for us on the way. We think we should get there by tomorrow night. Then we will send George in through the electric system. He will try to locate Mark and report his whereabouts to us. Then he'll create a diversion by shorting out their lights. That should give us a chance to get in and spirit Mark out in the confusion. With any luck, we'll get a good head start before they can reorganize. Family Rooster will fly back to summon you and other Good Guys to meet us and turn back any pursuit. If all goes well, we should have Mark back in three days." He took a deep breath, "If all goes well."

Keith took over. "While we're gone, we ask you to make it appear as if we are, in fact, hiding here. Our plan depends on complete surprise. And I want to thank you in advance for watching Todd for us while we're gone. Knowing he's safe here will make our job easier."

"But I don't want to be kept safe here," Todd shouted.

Keith ignored him. "Now that you have an idea of what we are doing, we need to cut this short. Darkness *is* falling."

Friendly Doctor stood up and walked to the front. "I want to start by saying that I'm relieved that you have a plan and that it sounds hopeful. That said, I want to let you know that I appreciate your desire for haste, but I also know something of the human as well as dinosaur makeup. I'm afraid that the old slogan 'Haste Makes Waste' could well apply here. I can see that you're tired, nearing the end of your rope. My opinion is that you would greatly increase your chances of success by getting a night and day to rest and then leaving tomorrow night."

"I agree," said Mr. Ty. "Also, don't you think that you'd be more able to convince the enemy of your intentions to stay here if you made yourselves quite visible for a day?"

Other dinosaurs nodded. Rick, Keith, Marc Monster, and the Lugu huddled, and George looked down from the light. Marc Monster said he was "raring to go," but the others looked at each other and saw the same weariness that Friendly Doctor had pointed out. After a few words and a signal from George, Keith announced a decision. "All right. We leave tomorrow night, and we rest tonight."

"Yes, *we* leave tomorrow," said Todd. But Rick just shook his head.

Back at the Brontos' house, Todd prepared for bed. For the first time on the trip he felt alone. He missed his bed at Grandma and Grandpa's. He missed being tucked in by his mother. *Maybe I'm not such a big Good Guy after all*, he thought.

He was sitting quietly by a grass-covered window that provided a good view looking out but was hard to spot from the outside. He jumped when he heard someone sneaking up behind him. Whirling and raising his fists, he relaxed when he saw Baby Bronto approaching and carrying something.

"You can sleep with my anky-bank tonight," Baby Bronto whispered. He held out a plush ankylosaurus, a toy that served as both a Teddy bear and a piggy bank.

Todd had heard of the attachment the baby dinosaurs had for their anky-banks. How could he ask such a favor? But he saw a pleading look in Baby Bronto's eyes. "Thanks," he said, reaching out to accept the offer.

"Tomorrow you can play with us," said Baby Bronto as he hurried back down the hall.

Todd lugged the anky-bank into the spare bedroom where he shared a single brontosaurus-sized bed with the rest of his group. He cuddled up next to the bank and felt comfortable. His body tingled with the cool heat of the salve. A refreshing breeze touched him now and then, and the soothing sounds of the lake shore—crickets, katydids, the occasional croaking of a bullfrog, the chirping of the spring peepers, the eerie laughter of a loon, and the lapping of tiny lake waves against the shore—lulled him to a peaceful sleep.

It would be the last he would enjoy for a while.

Chapter 9: A Day at the Lake

Long before Todd awoke the next morning, his companions and the good dinosaurs gathered to review their plans. For the most part, nothing had changed except for the delay of one day. Rick and Keith felt invigorated after the night's rest and agreed that the time lost had been worthwhile and that it increased their chances of success.

One item still hung in the balance: the question of Todd's participation. He had been determined to go along from the start, but Rick was reluctant to take him farther. "I already have one brother in danger," he said. "Todd will be safe here. He doesn't know what he would be getting into if he goes with us."

Marc Monster disagreed. "I understand your concern, but this might be the time he comes into his own as a Good Guy. Can you understand how he must feel having to hang around here with no power over what happens, worrying all the while?"

"Don't forget how I'll be worried all the while, not just about Mark, but also about Todd if he comes with us. This mission will be plenty dangerous, and Todd is so inexperienced."

"He has to get experienced sometime. He has a lot about him, and his heart is in this."

The debate went on for some time. Everyone agreed that Rick should make the final decision. He walked down to the lakeshore and sat for the best part of an hour before returning. Rick and Keith carried the news back to the Brontos', only to find that Todd was outside playing with the baby dinosaurs.

"It's probably best to let him enjoy himself for a while," said Keith. They walked to a shady spot near the lake where they joined Marc Monster and the Lugu for a refreshing nap.

Small voices invaded Todd's sleep, raising him step by step to waking. He rolled over and opened one eye. He saw a young plateosaurus and tyrannosaurus scamper away from the doorway. Closing the eye, he slipped back into a light doze until the voices again roused him. This time he sat up and stretched. He was alone in the room, but not for long. He no more than stood up when five young dinosaurs bounded in and danced around him.

"Come on out and play with us," said Baby Tri, and the other four echoed his request.

Mrs. Bronto, who had spent most of the morning trying to hold down the youngsters' enthusiasm, called in from the next room. "Not so fast, you five. Let our guest have breakfast first."

And breakfast he had. He did not know for certain what he was eating. It certainly was not Sugar Honey Crunchies, but he had to admit that he liked it. He took four servings. Each time he finished one, the baby dinosaurs wriggled in their places, only to disappointedly settle back as he took another.

At last Todd thanked Mrs. Bronto and stepped back from the table. No longer able to control themselves, the babies escorted him out the door. They each carried an anky-bank, and they shook them to show Todd how much money they had saved. The silver "gizzards" made much more noise than the paper "livers" (as dinosaurs name their money), and Todd congratulated them all for their thriftiness.

They made their way to a sandy side hill where they tunneled and constructed forts for their anky-banks until the sun rose above the hill's edge, beating down on them. Todd's forehead beaded up with sweat, and he fanned himself with a leafy branch.

"Let's go over to Friendly Doctor's," said Baby Tri.

"It's all right," said Todd. "I'm feeling fine, just a little hot."

"Oh, that's not it," said Baby Ty. "You'll see."

So, anky-banks in hand, they left the sand and climbed a trail. They waved at Family Paper Boy who was carving out the daily edition on a flat piece of sandstone. They shouted greetings to Jack whose legs stuck out from beneath the algae harvester he was repairing. Inside a nearby cave they found Friendly Doctor washing the breakfast dishes. "I'm a little late doing this," he apologized. "I had a meeting this morning."

Baby Steg set his anky-bank down. "Friendly Doctor, tell us a story."

Friendly Doctor looked at him and smiled. "All right. Just let me think of one while I finish these dishes." Then he saw that Todd was with the youngsters. He looked as if he wanted to tell Todd something, but he returned to his job.

When he finished, he closed his eyes briefly. Opening them, he went to his cupboard and prepared bread and blackberry jam for everyone. He led them outside and asked them to sit in a circle amidst a dandelion patch under a hazel tree.

"Once upon a time, five young dinosaurs...and a boy... went for a walk in the forest." The dinosaurs giggled and looked at Todd, their eyes wide and sparkling.

Friendly Doctor continued. "They had not gone far when they saw a freshly painted sign tacked up to a tree. The boy read it to them. It said, 'New Swimming Pool Now Open.' Underneath the words, an arrow pointed to a path leading into the woods.

"'That sounds like fun,' said the dinosaurs, and the boy agreed, so they followed the path. Every so often, another sign pointed them farther along the trail. They continued until they reached a clearing where two allosauruses, one gray and one brown, stood next to a huge kettle of water.'"

At the mention of the two allosauruses, Todd heard the babies whispering to one another, and he saw them frowning and shaking their heads.

"The two allosauruses smiled at them, but their smiles did not look friendly. 'Welcome to the new swimming pool,' said the gray one.

"'We are here to serve you,' said the brown one.

"The young dinosaurs looked the situation over. 'How come is there wood piled up under the swimming pool?' asked the young brontosaurus. 'It looks like you are going to have a fire.'

"'Why, of course we are,' said the gray allosaurus. 'This is a heated pool.'

"The young plateosaurus then asked, 'Why do you both have salt shakers in your hands?'

"The brown allosaurus answered, 'That is because some folks like the ocean experience. We salt the water so it is just like swimming off a tropic island beach.'

"The young stegosaurus asked, 'Why do you have carrots and onions piled around the pool?'

"'After a good swim,' said the gray allosaurus, 'many folks are hungry, so we have these healthy snacks ready for them. Not before you go in, of course. Then you would have to wait an hour to swim.'

"The young triceratops pointed at a huge iron cover lying near the pool. 'What is that for?' he asked.

"'That,' said the brown allosaurus, 'is a retractable roof. In case of rain we can put it over the pool so you won't get wet.'

"As he said this, both allosauruses tied napkins around their necks. The young tyrannosaurus asked, 'What are you wearing napkins for?'

"The gray one answered, 'These are not napkins. They are fancy neckties. Now that we are business tycoons with our own swimming pool, we need to dress with class. Now, don't you think it is time to go swimming?'

"The allosauruses dragged a ramp to the edge of the pool and gestured to the group. 'Last one in is a rotten trachodon,' they said.

"The young dinosaurs hesitated. Then the boy said, 'It is good to see such enterprising businessdinosaurs as you. Since you are getting your business going, we would feel guilty if we did not pay you for the service, don't you think?'

"The allosauruses looked at each other. Sly smiles crossed their faces, and drool hung from their sharp teeth. 'Well, we *do* usually charge two livers to swim here,' said the gray one.

"'And then there is sales tax,' said the brown one.

"The boy added, 'Of course, it would be inconsiderate of us not to leave a tip.'

"Now the allosauruses' feet danced merrily and drool rolled down their chins.   'Right you are,' said the brown one. 'That ought to come to about five livers apiece, give or take ten or fifteen.'

"'That only sounds fair,' said the boy. 'There is only one small problem, though. Our money is at home in our anky-banks. Can you wait for us to go get it?'

"The gray allosaurus winked at his partner. 'Certainly we will wait. I have a good idea. Why don't you bring your anky-banks along, and we will count out the money while you are swimming. Hurry back, but we will wait. Yes, we will wait.'

"The boy and the young dinosaurs left then. As far as I know, those allosauruses are waiting still. The end."

The baby dinosaurs erupted with laughter and cheering. Todd clapped along with them, and he understood why they had wanted to visit Friendly Doctor.

The cave man invited them to have lunch with him. Afterwards, they spent the rest of the day playing. When they finally broke up for supper, Todd realized that he had almost forgotten why he was there. He felt guilty for having so much fun while the Bad Guys held his brother hostage. He had begun to think he would be happy to stay with the dinosaurs after all, but when he thought of Mark, he felt selfish. "I *must* go," he whispered to himself.

Rick, Keith, Marc Monster, and the Lugu greeted Todd at the Brontos' door. "Mr. Bronto has prepared supper. You will want to eat a big one," said Keith.

"I want to go," said Todd.

"You are going," said Rick.

"But he's my brother, too. I want to…I am?" Todd's face lit up. "I'm going? I'm going!" He clapped his hands and jumped up and down.

If he had known what lay ahead, he might have thought otherwise.

Chapter 10: Hairy Jack

Night crept slowly across Blue Lake. The brighter stars peeped down upon it already, and their shyer cousins began to appear, one by one. The day's heat hung in the air as it does on humid summer evenings, and the residents of the lake welcomed a gentle zephyr that rustled the leaves and rippled the lake's surface.

Six travelers readied themselves for a cloaked departure from the tunnel leading to the Brontos' runway into the lake. Five of them carried floatation devices, and Keith had an extra, plus a flashlight sealed in a plastic bag. Inside the light, the sixth huddled nervously.

"Perfect," said Keith, looking out at the wavy surface of the water. "If we paddle carefully, our wake shouldn't be noticeable."

As the last purple hints of daylight left the sky, they bade farewell to the Brontos and others gathered to see them off. Creeping along the walls of the runway, they glided into the water, five figures staying as much below the surface as they could and one flashlight in a life preserver.

They propelled themselves slowly and silently out into the depths. The moon was a day or so past full, and Keith estimated that they would have three-fourths of an hour before it rose. During that time the dark would conceal them. Even the sharpest eye, if it spied anything at all, might take them for a flock of ducks or geese on a nocturnal excursion.

The cool of the water refreshed Todd after sweltering through the muggy day. He listened to the occasional twang of bullfrogs from their favorite lily pads along the lake's shallows. Far away a dog barked at some passing shadow. Todd started once at the cry of a nighthawk but otherwise heard only the light plash of their paddling.

A glow heralding the coming arrival of the moon spread wide across the eastern sky by the time they approached the far shore. The Lugu had already climbed out of the water when Todd felt something wrap around his leg. Recoiling, he gasped and churned the surface. Rick turned and shushed him, and Todd saw that he had entered a water lily bed and had merely kicked through a slippery stem. He reached shore without incident after that, but after sloshing among several more slimy, submerged vines, he silently vowed never to swim through water lilies again.

Rick helped him ashore and pressed a finger to his lips. They walked a hundred feet or so into the forest until they came to a downed tree, which made a good bench to sit on while they regrouped. Keith broke out the mosquito repellent, and he, Rick, and Todd applied it liberally. The Lugu unwrapped the flashlight, and George's voice squeaked, "Thank Heavens. I thought I was going to suffocate."

After Rick reminded everyone to keep their voices down, Todd asked, "How long does it take to get to Bad Guy headquarters from here?"

Keith answered. "If we marched directly along roads and trails, we could get there in three hours. Of course, we can't do that. We'll be taking hidden ways and circling around a lot. We don't want to draw attention to ourselves. This will probably take a lot of extra time, just like our trip to the dinosaurs. I'm hoping we can reach there about this time tomorrow. That includes getting some sleep on the way."

Todd wondered whether he would have been better off staying at Blue Lake.

Once their clothes stopped dripping, they moved out. The Lugu knew the country well, so he led. Marc Monster followed and carried George in the flashlight. Keith came next, then Todd, and finally Rick. At first, they picked their way through the woods, trying to avoid patches of prickly ash, wild raspberries, gooseberries, and other thorny plants. At one point the Lugu led them in a wide arc around a small clearing where he knew poison ivy grew.

Soon they felt the ground turning mushy under their feet. The sound of many frogs singing rose louder with every step. They stopped for a few minutes while the Lugu scouted to the right and left. At last he returned and announced, "I've found the path, folks."

They followed him a hundred yards to the left where he turned and seemed to head into a swamp. Todd saw Keith enter a tiny slit in the tall grass. Not much of a path, he thought, but he soon felt solid ground beneath his feet.

Keith stopped and whispered, "This is good. It doesn't look like anyone has been through here in weeks."

The lightning bugs (as Keith sometimes called the fireflies) sparkled as brightly here as any place along their route. Todd noticed a dim humming sound that gradually got louder. This time he knew its source, and he was thankful for the repellent Keith had brought. The thought of the swarming mosquitoes made him stop to slap at an imagined itch. Rick reminded him to try to stay closer to Keith.

Rick was having second thoughts about the wisdom of bringing Todd. He constantly needed to spur him forward. "Try to keep up with Keith," he would say. "Stick together. Don't dawdle. Keep up the pace." Determined to prove his worthiness, Todd did his best to press on.

As time passed, the trail grew clearer. The Lugu stopped and warned everyone of the need for utmost caution. "Someone comes this way at times," he said. "I doubt if anyone will tonight, but it's best to be wary, folks. Bad Guys may be about, and we are also coming to the edge of Hairy Jack's domain."

"Who's Hairy Jack?" asked Todd. "A Bad Guy?"

"He's not a Bad Guy, but we don't want to run into him," Keith said. "He's just as dangerous as any of them and more so than most. The good news is that they don't like to come around his lands either."

Keith brought out a canteen, and everyone took a drink. Todd thought he would rather see Jack the dinosaur than this Hairy Jack. Marc Monster sat down next to him.

"Don't be worrying about Hairy Jack. He's no match for this group," he said. Then he added, "I see you are having a little trouble keeping up. Why don't you let me take your pack for a while? It wouldn't be making much difference for me at all." Todd started to decline, but he remembered what Rick had been saying, and he accepted Marc's offer.

They arose again and took to the trail. It was past midnight, and the moon floated high in the sky, although they saw little of it except when marshes opened breaks in the trees. They came to a place where the path ran by such a marsh. Glancing toward the opening, Todd noticed a light that seemed to grow and move, first toward him and then away again. "Is that lightning bugs?" he asked Rick.

Rick peered at the light. "No. It's more like a lantern. I don't know what it is." He saw fear in Todd's eyes. "I don't think it's Hairy Jack. Let's ask Keith." He called to Keith in a loud stage whisper, and Keith halted the troop.

"It's best not to pay any attention to that," Keith said. "I've only seen it a few times. Maybe the Lugu can help me out, but I think it's a will o' the wisp."

"Me, too," said the Lugu.

"What's that?" asked Todd.

Keith said, "It is just what you see, a light in the swamp. Some people say they are spirits trying to lead people into the bogs until they are hopelessly lost. Whatever they are, they give me the creeps. Like I said, pay it no attention. Come on. Let's keep going."

The Lugu led them on down the trail. He came to a point where it forked. Without hesitation, he took the left branch. Marc Monster and Keith followed suit, but Todd and Rick lagged behind, fascinated by the light. "Go ahead, Todd," Rick said, nudging him forward.

Todd went on, but Rick could not help taking another look at the light. It flickered and flared up slightly. Rick almost thought he saw someone waving at him. The will o' the wisp, or whatever it was, wanted him to follow it. Maybe it knew something. Maybe it could help him find Mark. Maybe it knew a shortcut. Rick took three halting steps toward it, and it seemed to move away down the swamp. He walked several more steps and stopped again. He thought he saw it wave again and move farther away. He must follow. The light entranced him, and his only choice was to obey.

He was about to continue when a foul odor wrenched him back to reality. He immediately plugged his nose, and he remembered Keith's advice. Looking down, he saw a black pool before him, stagnant and reeking. He backed away in disgust. The lantern came closer, but he had broken free from its spell. Whirling, he hurried up the trail and looked back no more.

Rick took several minutes to catch up with the others. He left the swampy area behind and entered a thick section of woods. He could barely make out the trail in front of his feet. When he finally heard his companions moving ahead of him, he sighed in relief. How foolish he'd been. It was not like him to lose his focus and jeopardize the mission. It felt good to be back on the move. They were making good progress, and Todd seemed to be moving along much better than he had earlier.

Who knows how long they marched along this way? And who knows why Keith suddenly stopped and turned to tell Todd something? But when he did, he saw Rick, and Rick saw him, and neither saw Todd. Rick dropped to his knees, his mouth open and his arms spread wide. "Is Todd ahead of you?" he asked in a weak voice.

Keith shook his head.

"Where is he?" Rick said, a little too loud for conditions. "Where is he?"

The Lugu and Marc Monster rushed back to see what was happening. Rick looked at Marc and shouted, "I shouldn't have listened to you. Now he's gone." He shoved him aside.

Marc Monster's head dropped, and his shoulders sagged. Keith ran to Rick and put his arm on his shoulder, but Rick ripped away. Rick grabbed his head with both hands and leaned against a tree, trying to put the events of the last few minutes in order. The Lugu stared at the scene in shock. George peeked out of the flashlight. Marc Monster sat down next to another tree and muttered, "I'm sorry," over and over.

So much had happened to Rick in the last few days that he thought he would burst. But he was a Good Guy with Good Guy training, and he fought to compose himself. He looked at Marc Monster, also with his head buried in his hands. *How much had they been through together? How many times had he trusted Marc?* He breathed deeply and forced himself to be composed. "It's me," he said. "It's me who has lost two brothers in four days."

He went to Marc and knelt beside him. "I'm the one who should be sorry," he said. "You showed faith in Todd, and he proved himself. He was able to walk away from the light in the swamp, and I was not. I'm sorry, old friend. I should never blame you." He reached out his hand, and Marc Monster took it.

"But I'm still sorry," said Marc.

Rick nodded and turned his face away. Then he stood and faced the group. "Give me half an hour. If I am not back, go on. I'll try to catch up later." Under his breath he added, "And it better be with Todd."

"You are not looking alone," said Keith. As one, the entire group ran back down the trail.

###

When Rick pushed Todd away from the will o' the wisp, Todd moved up the trail, but the call of the light still gripped him. Looking behind him as he went, he virtually backed along the path. If he noticed the fork in it, he never gave it a thought, so obsessed on the light was he. At last it vanished behind a clump of trees, and he was free of its power. He quickened his pace and strode forward.

Several minutes passed, and he saw no sign of the others. The forest had never felt so lonely and deserted. Even the mosquitoes vanished. The hooting of an owl off to his left assured him that the woods were not quite empty, but he strained his eyes and ears for some sign of Keith.

No such sights or sounds reached him until he half imagined footsteps behind him. Sighing with relief, he waited for Rick to catch him. "He will probably tell me I'm going too slow again," he said to himself, but he would even welcome a reprimand at that point. "I'll show him I'm trying," he whispered, and he walked a little faster.

Now he was sure he heard steps. They sounded clearer by the second. A strange shiver flashed up and down his spine for no apparent reason. He laughed to himself and thought about how he would tell Rick about it. *Only another minute or two and I'll be able to do just that*, he reassured himself.

A strange grunt caught him off guard. Rick never sounded like that. Glancing back, he saw Rick approaching, a shadowy form in the darkness. Another glance froze him in horror. The form was not Rick's, not Rick's at all. He saw long, thin arms and longer, gangly legs like pipe cleaners attached to a potato body. Not Rick's at all.

Now Todd ran, trying to cry out but unable to make a sound. The trail, difficult to walk along in the dark, became impossible to follow at a dead run. He crashed into a bush and scrambled to get up. He found the trail, only to lose it again a few steps later. Scanning the darkness, he saw what appeared to be the way, but as he turned to run to it the pipe cleaner arms closed around him.

Slight as they appeared, those arms gripped him like steel clamps. A hand, much too large for those arms groped for his face and covered his mouth. A throaty voice, accompanied by a blast of some of the worst breath Todd had ever smelled (or tasted, for that matter, and he could) said, "No yell." Then it broke off into an extended cackle.

The creature eyed Todd in the dark and then carried him to an opening near a small lake. In the moonlight, Todd made out a strange, round face studying his own. It sported a nose several sizes too big, a mouth full of triangular teeth separated by gaps partially filled by oozing green matter, and ears like a Mickey Mouse hat that had sagged to both sides. It was dressed in loose-fitting deerskin and wore moccasins of birch bark.

The feature that Todd noticed most, however, was the hair. Long hair hung from its head in front of and behind its ears which themselves sprouted tufts of it. It had hairy arms, hairy legs, hairy shoulders, hairy hands, hairy fingers. From anywhere the deerskin left bare hung hair, long and straight as a yak's. Its eyebrows hung precariously down halfway over its eyes. It had a scraggly beard but no mustache. No matter. The hair growing out from its nose covered its lip just as well.

Surely this was the creature called Hairy Jack. Todd thought of asking it (or him) if that was his name, but he did not dare.

Hairy Jack continued to scrutinize Todd. He sniffed at him, poked at his stomach, felt the muscles on his arms and legs, and licked his cheeks, giving him another jolt of fetid breath in the process. Then he sat back as if to rest, his hand never relaxing its grip.

Todd was beginning to hope Hairy Jack would fall asleep when the creature's head popped up abruptly. He poked a long, hairy finger into his ear and twisted it. He tilted his head, mouth in a grimace. Then Todd heard something. Someone called out from the trail behind them, and soon Todd could make out what the person was calling—his name.

Hairy Jack clamped a hand over Todd's mouth again and hauled him up into the woods where he flopped down behind a clump of brush. The voices drew closer and passed. Todd recognized them as Keith's and Marc Monster's. Hairy Jack's huge paw prevented him from answering their cries, even had he dared to try. In fact, he feared he would not be able to draw another breath, so tightly was his face covered.

The hand relaxed slightly when Keith and Marc passed, but Hairy Jack remained in his position. A few minutes later, Todd felt it tightening again. Moments later, he heard the same two voices pass in the other direction. Hairy Jack waited, unmoving, for a long time. A half-hour? An hour? Todd could not tell, but the time seemed endless. End it did, however, and at last Hairy Jack got up and carried Todd, unable to break that grip as hard as he tried, away through the woods and swamps.

Chapter 11: Gooseberry

Rick, Keith, the Lugu, and Marc Monster raced back to the spot where they had seen the will o' the wisp, hoping that they would meet Todd straggling along. The Lugu suggested that Todd may have taken the wrong fork in the trail, so Keith and Marc volunteered to search in that direction. The Lugu backtracked down the trail in case Todd might have gone back toward Blue Lake in the confusion.

Meanwhile, Rick took the flashlight and George to investigate the immediate vicinity. He pointed the light at the spot where the will o' the wisp had appeared. "Take that," he said. He panned the ground for any sign, and the light showed footprints ahead, but he recognized them as his own. Coming to the stagnant pool, he saw the layer of scum covering it like a foul carpet. He was relieved to see no sign of disturbance, no hint that someone might have splashed into it. He called Todd's name repeatedly and shone the light all around until Keith and Marc Monster returned, unsuccessful.

The Lugu came huffing and puffing up the trail a short time later. "How ya doin', folks?" he asked between pants. They shook

101

their heads.

"What are we going to do?" asked Keith.

"Keep looking until we find him," said Marc Monster.

"No," said Rick with a wave of his hand and a look that said he meant it. "We set out to rescue Mark, and we can't turn away from that. This has cost us enough time already. I'm going to do what I suggested earlier. I'll stay and search for him. You four will have to go on and complete the mission. Maybe Todd and I will catch up with you, but even if we don't…." He paused, took a deep breath, and swallowed. "Even if we don't, please save Mark."

The others stood silently for a moment. Marc Monster looked as if he wanted to say something, but no words came out. They hugged Rick. Even George popped out and stretched his arms as far around Rick's neck as he could. Then, with a wave, they were gone.

The city of Gooseberry had been the dream of an east coast speculator some time in the second half of the 19th century. A clever con man had fueled the dream by selling him the rights to a marvelous tract of land.

"The railroad's comin' through, and I've heard tell that the north-south line and the east-west line will be meetin' there," said the con man. "I wish I had the funds to develop it, but since I don't, I'll take what small profit I can by sellin' the property. You look to be just the man to turn it into the thriving little community—dare I say gold mine?—that it could be."

The speculator saw nothing but dollar signs. Had he actually visited the tract, he would have seen nothing but swamps and scraggly forest. He definitely would not have seen any railroads. But he did not visit, and the visions of dollar signs prevailed.

Congratulating himself on the incomparable bargain he had negotiated with the con man, he commissioned a crew to construct the core of his new Camelot. They built a store, a saloon, a jailhouse, and a few simple dwellings. *Once people start to fill them in, the newcomers will build their own houses, hiring my crew, of course*, he thought.

Within a very short time the truth emerged, and the speculator's dreams abandoned Gooseberry, as did its few residents, for more profitable enterprises. By the time of our story, only the jailhouse, the lone building made of stone in Gooseberry, remained. Everything else had fallen down, rotted, and sunk into the swamps. The world had long since forgotten it—all the world, that is, except for its one inhabitant.

###

First light was still a good two hours away when Hairy Jack reached Gooseberry with his prize. He flung open the jailhouse door and tossed Todd onto the floor. Todd heard the jingling of keys a moment before being shoved through an opening. A door slammed after him, and when he reached for it, he felt steel bars. Todd was a prisoner in the single cell of the Gooseberry jail.

He found a bed in the back of the cell and flopped down on it. Before long, he heard rhythmic breathing as Hairy Jack fell asleep in the jailer's office. The peace was brief. Hairy Jack was a notorious snorer.

Naturally enough, Todd did not sleep for the rest of the night. He pictured his bedroom at his grandparents' house. He longed for another night at the Brontos'. What he would give to be holding an anky-bank! But he mostly thought about getting away.

Perhaps his friends would find him. Maybe Hairy Jack would release him in the morning. He doubted that. Something inside gnawed at him, telling him that he must help himself. As much as he thought of solutions, nothing came to him. He fell into that pattern that comes to people in the middle of the night when all is dark including that part of our minds holding our hopes and fears. Curling his body into a ball, he tried to cover bleak images with happy memories. So he spent the rest of the night.

Dawn revealed the shape of Todd's prison. Through the bars
he saw an ancient wooden table and chair. Beyond that, Hairy Jack
snored on a cot near a broken out window. The day's first sunlight
streaming through that window fell on a curious object in the corner,
an old-fashioned upright piano. Had Todd known the history of
Gooseberry, he might have guessed that it had once played honky-
tonk music for the sparse gatherings in the town saloon. Next to it
sat a brass spittoon, now tarnished and green. The rest of the room,
the old jailer's office, was decorated in early, middle, and late
rubbish style, hung generously with cobwebs. In places, small
beams of light sneaked in through rust-enlarged nail holes in the
building's tin roof.

His eyes turned to his own cell, and he stood up instantly. By
all appearances even the bedbugs had long ago moved out in search
of a more wholesome neighborhood. He scanned his skin, half
expecting to see a plague of foul, creeping things hatching from
beneath it.

Hairy Jack's snoring, which had been a feverish growl like
the grinders at the Vermillion Falls feed mill, now burst forth like
nearby thunder, and he abruptly woke up. He cleared his throat and
spat on the wall before lumbering outside.

Todd hoped he was leaving for the day, but minutes later he returned carrying an earthen crock. Setting it on the table, he pulled a ring of keys from a back pocket and opened the door to Todd's cell. He motioned for Todd to move to the back of the compartment, a needless gesture since Todd had already backed as far away as possible. Hairy Jack took the crock from the table and placed it on the cell floor before shutting the door with a resounding clank and returning the keys to his pocket. Todd noticed that the top of the key ring projected out of it. He thought of trying to grab it, but he realized that even if he could, Hairy Jack would easily overpower him before he could get anywhere.

When his captor again went outside, Todd crept forward and checked out the crock. It was full of water. Through his ordeal he had almost forgotten his needs. Now a terrible thirst rushed over him, and yet he did not drink. Algae floated atop the cloudy liquid. Mosquito larvae wriggled from the top to the bottom and back, and a rancid smell rose from it. No, his thirst would have to be many times worse to drink that water.

Hairy Jack returned and went straight to the piano. He started playing, if you could call such discord playing. Such indignities have rarely been inflicted upon the voice of an instrument. As he banged away, his body ground and writhed as if in extreme agony. Todd plugged his ears.

Suddenly the music changed. A sprightly, catchy, if slightly repetitive tune burst forth. Hairy Jack's body bounced, danced, and shook to the rhythm. He punctuated the end of each repetition by kicking the spittoon with a clang. Despite himself, Todd's toes started tapping, and he felt his head and shoulders bobbing with the music.

Just as suddenly as it had begun, the melody ended, and the writhing resumed, but Todd never forgot the moment. For the time being, however, ear-plugging time returned. The cacophony seemed never-ending. How long could even Hairy Jack stand it?

Then, abruptly, it stopped. Hairy Jack turned his head slowly. His enormous snout sniffed the air, and his ears twitched. He grunted one word, "Rat." As quickly as a Bad Guy might pounce on a penny, he sprang into a corner where he thrust his arms and upper body under a pile of rubble. Emerging with the rat in hand, he consumed it in three bites. He wiped his mouth with the back of his furry arm and howled with glee. He danced five turns around the room and sat down with a resounding belch.

Todd found himself wedged into the corner again. He gasped for air after unconsciously holding his breath through the spectacle he had just witnessed. Disgusted as he was, a plan sprouted in his brain.

Hairy Jack settled into his chair, a contented look on his face. Todd waited until peace returned to the old jailhouse to execute his idea. Was he sweating from the heat of the sun on the tin roof, or had it something to do with his trembling hands? He slipped a dark object out of his pocket and placed it under the bed. Then he leaped to the door of his cell and yelled, "Eew, eew, there's a rat in here! Eew, a rat! Help!"

Hairy Jack jammed the key into the lock before his upset chair hit the floor. With a quick scan of the room he sighted the rat's tail jutting out from beneath the bed. He dove for it. In that instant, Todd snatched the key from the door and slammed it shut. With a look of dismay, Hairy Jack pulled back from under the bed with a rat-tailed bow tie in his hand. His dismay turned to anger when he saw Todd drop the key to his locked cell onto the table.

Todd bolted out the door. He was free. He thanked Dr. Rankato's persistence. The fifty cents the bow tie had cost him would have bought many baseball cards in those days, but what a small price for his freedom.

A moment later he knew he was not completely free. He stood in Hairy Jack's front yard surrounded by Bad Guy Country.

Somewhere out there walked his five companions, but where? At the same time, hundreds of enemies prowled the land. Which way led to his friends, or home, or to any kind of safety? And which way led to—no, he wouldn't think of that.

In addition, the sun beat down more intensely than it had even during the last two muggy days. The humidity hung so thick in the air that he hardly knew whether to run or to swim. Such air made breathing difficult.

A buzzing sound and a sharp, painful pinch on his neck told him that the deer flies were busy in Gooseberry that day. He slapped at the spot and looked up to see a squadron of the miserable pests circling his head. Keith had told him that deer flies preferred the sun, but he knew that entering the forest would merely exchange their unwelcome company for that of mosquitoes.

Standing bewildered, he looked around him, and his mind cleared. In his joy and confusion, he had barely noticed the sound of a stormy rampage, and now he took heed of it—the wrathful frenzy of Hairy Jack. The woods offered a chance. Standing still offered none.

His eyes sought anything resembling a trail over solid ground. When he spied one, he followed the lead of so many potential settlers of old and took leave of Gooseberry with all possible haste.

Chapter 12: Nothing For the Skeleton Who Has Everything

Todd dashed down the path, really little more than a deer trail, until his breath failed him. As he stopped, bent over with hands on hips trying to catch his breath, his dry mouth reminded him of his need for water. His stomach grumbled and growled, demanding breakfast. Even in the woods, the heat and humidity sapped his strength. Knowing that he needed to conserve his energy, he slackened his pace. This gave the mosquitoes a chance to hover around him, so he spent a great deal of that saved energy slapping at them.

He was feeling miserable and more than a little discouraged when a welcome sound reached his ears. A faint trickle off to the right hinted at fresh water. To his delight, he found a spring bubbling icy-cold from the side of a small rise. The crystal clear liquid poured out and collected in a natural basin before running off to join some larger stream or to dump into a marsh. Todd knelt before the basin and drank. Then he splashed his face, arms, and body. He sat back for a minute and drank again. He wished he had not let Marc Monster carry his canteen for him, but for now the spring invigorated him, and he drank a third time. Now he moved more briskly, but with his thirst quenched, his hunger intensified. So it was that when the trees parted briefly and he saw the patch of wild strawberries, he let down his guard to rush out and gorge himself. As quickly as he could pick the berries, he stuffed them into his mouth. Sugar Honey Crunchies never tasted so exquisite.

"Hey, little buddy, you look hungry," said a voice from just inside the shadow of the trees.

Todd's head jerked up, and he stopped picking. A large-boned skeleton stepped out of the woods. "Hey, little buddy, why don't you come over to my place? I've got everything."

"Who are you?" asked Todd. His eyes squinted together under a frown, and his legs tensed, ready to run.

"Aw, why ask questions like that, little buddy? Can't you see I'm trying to help you out? You just looked hungry, and I've got everything you could possibly want to eat at my place."

"Do you have Sugar Honey Crunchies?"

"Oh, sure. I've got that sugar and crunchy honey. I told you. I've got everything."

"Do you have bacon and eggs?"

"You bet I do."

"How about toast with persimmon jelly?"

"Sure, little buddy. I've got lots of that. I put up that percinnamon jelly myself every fall."

"Who are you? What's your name?"

"All right, all right. Since you have to know, my name's Kerm, Kerm Skeleton, but you can call me Uncle Kermy. Now, like I said, little buddy, you should come over to my place. I've got everything. Do you like games?"

"Sure."

"Well, then, I've got every game they ever made. I've got this big field where you can play baseball or football."

"Can you play shoulder ball?"

"You bet, little buddy. We play that all the time. How about fishing? Do you like to fish? I've got a lake at my place, and it's plumb full of every kind of fish you could name. We can just sit on the shore and catch one with every cast. When you get tired of fishing, you can go swimming. I've got a nice, big raft you can swim out to and dive off."

"Do you have bass in your lake?"

"Yep, I do."

"Walleyes, catfish, muskies, bluegills, northerns?"

"Yep, yep, yep, yep, and yep."

"Do you have southerns?"

"Yep. Lots of them."

"Do you have tarpon?"

"Oh, yeah, little buddy. When the grass gets all dewy we put a tarp on it so you can sit there and not get wet."

"Are you a Bad Guy?"

"Now there you go asking foolish questions again. Aren't you old enough to judge for yourself, little buddy? I just want to be your Uncle Kermy."

Todd stood for a minute without speaking. Then he remembered Friendly Doctor's story. "Your place sounds great, Uncle Kermy, but I'd feel guilty taking advantage of all that without paying."

Kerm Skeleton smiled at him, an awkward, forced smile. "You really don't have to pay, little buddy. I'm just doing this out of the goodness of my heart. Of course, it does cost me a lot to keep all the stuff I have. So how much you got?"

"Oh, I don't have any money on me. I left it in the car. I'll go get it."

"Sounds good, little buddy. I'll come with you."

"Great," said Todd. "Then you can meet my friends. I'm not old enough to drive, you know."

Kerm halted. "Uh, what friends you talking about? Are they little like you?"

"No. I'm traveling with the Good Gugu and Cuckoo and a few good giants. Come on. I'm sure they would love to meet a buddy of mine like you are."

Kerm backed up a step. "You really don't need to give me any money, little buddy." Kerm scratched his chin. "Uh, *how* much you got?"

"Only about fifty dollars or so."

"Hmm," said Kerm. "I really just wanted to have one little buddy for now. You know, so I can really get to know you. While we are having all that fun we'll be having we can talk about what your other friends like. Then we can have a big party for them later. They can all come over to my place then. But for now, if you want to go get that money, I'll wait here."

"Great idea," said Todd. "They'll be so excited."

"Oh, no, no. Don't tell them about it yet. Let's make it be a big surprise later. They'll be so happy and proud of you."

"Are you sure?"

"Certainly, little buddy. There's nothing more fun than a surprise party. You can pop out of a big cake for them. Did I tell you I've got lots of big cakes? I've got everything at my place."

"Well, all right. If you say so, I won't tell them. The car is a little ways from here. I should be back in about an hour."

"Wonderful, little buddy. Then we'll go to my place. Remember, I've got everything, little buddy. And mum's the word."

"You've got it, Uncle Kermy," said Todd as he headed down the trail, waving as he went. To himself, however, he whispered, "Dumb's the word."

He hurried along, wanting to put as much ground between himself and Kerm as possible in the next hour. The strawberries had given him some strength, but he had to admit that the bacon and eggs Kerm had mentioned sure sounded tasty.

He figured he had walked for more than an hour when his eyes started to droop. The effects of the day's heat and the lack of sleep weighed heavily on him. Finding a bed of soft moss in the shade of a tall oak tree, he threw himself down "for a short rest." He heard the songs of birds around him. Somewhere, a woodpecker tapped away, busily searching for grubs. The scent of some kind of blossoms swept past his nose. Todd's eyes closed.

He had been napping for some time when the hand grabbed his shoulder and shook him.

Chapter 13: The Road to Headquarters

When Rick left the others, he took only what he needed: a little food, a canteen of water, and a bottle of mosquito repellent. He had not expected to get any sleep, and on that matter he was correct. Roaming far and wide all night, ever vigilant for Bad Guys while searching for Todd, he came to Gooseberry midway through the next day.

He scouted the area carefully before warily approaching the jailhouse. Even Rick respected Hairy Jack's strength. When he approached the building, he heard Hairy Jack grumbling inside. Freezing for a moment, Rick pressed on as the grumbling continued. He reached the window and slowly raised his head to peek inside, half expecting Hairy Jack to grab it at any minute.

But Hairy Jack was not preparing an ambush. He was in the lockup, diligently trying to snag keys off a table with a stick that appeared to be pieced together and tied with material that resembled a bow tie in some places and a rat's tail in others. Rick could see that Hairy Jack would not succeed yet, but he also saw more stick material in the cell, so he quietly retreated. *Had Todd something to do with this?*

He set off again, this time combing the land in the general direction of Bad Guy headquarters, hoping that if his brother had been in Gooseberry he would have known enough to go south. On he went for hours, twice narrowly avoiding Bad Guys out for mischief in the forest. Once he heard grumbling from a clearing. Cautiously approaching, he recognized Kerm Skeleton. He was pacing back and forth between two trees. "If he isn't back in ten minutes, I'm leaving," Kerm muttered. Rick backed off and sneaked away.

Around mid-afternoon he saw something curled up under an oak tree. He looked all around and stole up to it. "Please just be sleeping," he said under his breath. He reached out and shook it.

Todd awoke, swinging his fists. Rick grabbed them, and Todd recognized him. Putting his finger to his lips, Rick started laughing, silently but joyously, and he hugged his brother.

Keith, Marc Monster, the Lugu, and George progressed slowly and deliberately. Their movement demanded secrecy more than speed at this point. They met no resistance during the night. Shortly before dawn they found a small hollow close by the trail, and they slept there for three or four hours.

In the morning they turned south, having looped far west of their destination. Here hills, open fields, and pastures interrupted the forest. They had to take long detours to stay under cover of the trees. Each of them often caught the others looking back in hopes of seeing Rick and Todd.

"I wish we could leave them some kind of a sign," Keith said.

"Unfortunately," said Marc Monster, "it would also say, 'Here we are, Bad Guys.'"

They reached the corner of a field and had taken only a few steps into the woods when they heard movement ahead. Falling on their hands and knees, they crawled up to a line of brush. Keith parted the leaves and saw three figures moving across the trail ahead: a doe and twin fawns still wearing their baby spots. He smiled and winked at the others who were also watching the deer.

A minute or more passed while they gazed, motionless, at the animals. Then a light breeze blew over them toward the deer. The doe raised her head. George, craning his neck to get a better view, slipped from the top of the flashlight, grasping at branches as he fell with a plunk. The doe's tail popped up, flashing white, and she bounded into the trees, closely followed by the fawns and their tiny flags of tails.

"That is always a sight I enjoy," said Marc Monster.

"Me, too," said the Lugu.

"It's good to find somebody out here who's not an enemy," said George as he climbed back on board.

"That breeze felt good, too," said Marc Monster. "The air has been dead all day."

Keith nodded but said nothing. He was thinking about the doe's signal to her family. *Signs do not have to be written*, he thought.

Rick and Todd sat munching on sandwiches from Rick's pack, sandwiches sent by their mother and grandmother. Todd would have wandered off into thoughts of home, but Rick pumped him for the full story of his adventures since their separation. He praised Todd for his handling of both encounters, but he frowned during the story of Kerm Skeleton.

"If he puts two and two together and reports to their headquarters, our cover is blown," he said as he packed up the lunch. "Come on, Todd. We need speed more than secrecy now."

He led Todd off their path and went weaving back and forth to avoid the underbrush. "This doesn't seem to be the quick way to go," said Todd.

"Stay with me," Rick said.

Soon the brush opened, and Todd saw a gravel road. "Are we going to walk down the road?" he asked.

"That, or close to it. If we are lucky, the Bad Guys won't see us. They aren't particularly fond of hanging out near roads, at least not in the middle of the afternoon. It's a chance we'll have to take."

Todd remembered Rick, Keith, and Mark peering warily from cars whenever they traveled around dusk or early evening. "That's when the Bad Guys are most active," they had told him.

Rick scanned the scene. "This won't be much good if they are watching from the trees, but it's all I can do." With a deep breath he stepped onto the shoulder of the road, and Todd followed.

They had jogged several hundred feet when Rick stopped Todd with his hand. "Car," he said. They dropped into the ditch and waited. A vehicle approached along the road behind them, moving slowly as if searching for something or someone. Todd held his breath. The car got closer, and they heard a familiar sound, the putt-putt-putt of a Model A pickup.

Rick leaped back onto the road and waved it down. The driver waved back and smiled. "Need a lift?" he asked.

Rick returned the smile and climbed into the front seat. He shook hands with the driver. "We sure do! It's good to see you, Dr. Rankato." Todd settled in beside him.

Dr. Rankato returned the pleasantries and looked at Todd. "Nice to see you again, too, young fella'. Have you had a chance to wear that tie yet?"

Todd's face turned red. He had skipped over the part about the rat-tailed bow tie when recounting his adventures to Rick. Now his brother looked at him curiously. "I, uh, gave it to a friend as a present," he said.

"That's a mighty fine thing to do," replied Dr. Rankato. "Of course, there's plenty more where that came from. I might just say that many's the customer who buys one for each day of the week plus one for special events. That's why we've got this special going. Just for this week they are fifty cents apiece or eight for four dollars."

Rick elbowed Todd lightly in the ribs. "I'm afraid we're just out for a walk today," he said. "We really didn't bring any money along."

A fleeting glum look crossed Dr. Rankato's face, but his normal good cheer quickly returned. "Now, now, you know a body's no good if he can't help out a friend once in a while. Do you think all I ever do is try to sell things? No, I say it's good to have the company. So what are a couple of lads like you doing here afoot?"

Todd looked at Rick. He knew it was best to let his older brother do the talking. "Oh, we are out on a kind of adventure, and we are trying to catch up with some friends."

"Well then, I hope you boys like it hot. What say, is it hot enough for you?" Rick and Todd made fanning motions with their hands, and Dr. Rankato continued. "Weatherman says it's the hottest, muggiest day of the year. You boys ought to pick out one of the lakes around here and go swimming. Say, if you don't have any trunks along, I've got some direct from the Riviera. French government surplus. Got some with pictures of Moody Mouse on them. He's big in France, you know. Oh, that's right, you didn't bring any money. Say, I could sell you some on credit and stop in tomorrow in the forenoon for payment."

Rick shook his head. "Sorry. We won't have time to swim today."

As they rode along, the road wove in and out among lakes, ponds, and marshes. For a while hills rose up on the north side, but now they came out of the forest onto a flat prairie. They reached a T intersection with a paved road. "Which way you boys going?" asked Dr. Rankato.

"South," said Rick.

"Fine, fine. That's my way, too. Adventure, you say? I just happen to have a box of books written by my good friend Professor Gelb. *Zoolatracs in the Old Gelb Mine*, it's called. High adventure. On special this week, too."

"It really is hot, isn't it?" said Rick.

"Hot, hot, yes. The weatherman said we might get a storm out of it. He said that ought to cool it down some and take the humidity out of the air. Always said, 'It's not the heat. It's the humidity.' Real good time to go swimming before it storms, you know. Say, you ever been on the beach, barefoot, and your toes look bad? I just got in a shipment of automatic toenail shiners. Not the old kind. These are this year's models with the rotating brushes. Gives your nails that sculpted look. It's the biggest thing to hit the Riviera since artificial shark fins. I don't suppose…."

"Here's our stop," Rick interrupted. "Thanks a lot for the ride. You're a real life saver."

"You sure you want to get out here? They's nothing around."

As they had traveled south, the road had reentered the woods. Now Rick pointed to an opening in the weeds on the east side and said, "I think that's where our friends went." He and Todd climbed

out of the pickup and waved goodbye to Dr. Rankato who waved
back and drove away.

"So you bought a tie," Rick said as they plunged back into
the woods. "Did you pay fifty cents? That would buy a lot of
baseball cards."

"That's what I thought, too," said Todd. "I really didn't want
a rat-tailed bow tie, but you know how he goes on. Actually, it
turned out to be pretty handy."

Rick nodded, knowingly.

They followed a trail for about half a mile before they saw a
large lake through the trees to the north. A car passed by on the road
to the south, and they heard it bend around a corner, heading north
on another road just ahead.

"There's a farm up there, and the road in to it is the last one
we will have to cross," whispered Rick. "We'll have to be careful.
The farmer has had some trouble with the Bad Guys, and he might
not be too hospitable to visitors popping out of the woods."

Minutes later they came to a field. Hoping to make good
time by following around its edge, Rick led Todd under the fence
and along the outside of a row of young, green oat sprouts. They
had almost reached the end of the field when a dog started barking.
Running for the far corner, Todd looked back and saw the farmer just

as he fired a shotgun into the air. "Next one will be in your pants. Now git!" he yelled.

Rick and Todd crawled under the fence and darted into the woods, not stopping until they reached the edge of an open pasture. There they sat down, gasping for breath.

Rick took off his shirt and fanned himself with it. "I'm going to hate to put this soaking thing back on," he said.

"Why didn't you tell him who we are?" asked Todd.

"Sometimes discretion is the better part of valor," said Rick.

"What?"

"What I'm saying is that shotgun may have done the talking first. He's just happy we're gone."

They sat in the shade of an elm tree, catching their breath and drinking from the canteen. Rick passed the mosquito repellent to Todd and looked at the sky. He pointed to a dark line just above the western horizon. "There's weather coming," he said. "We'd best move on."

As they stood up, his eyes fell on a pile of weeds, torn up and lying on a nearby cow path. Approaching it, he saw that they were arranged in the rough form of an arrow. "Keith was here, and he went that way," he said, pointing to the east and scuffing away the arrow with his foot, "and not too long ago. These weeds are not wilting yet."

"How do you know it was Keith?" asked Todd.

"See what kind of weeds they are? Pineapple weeds. Keith loves them."

Todd's face brightened. "I know," he said as he squeezed a bud and savored its sweet fragrance.

Chapter 14: The Storm

Keith and his companions had almost reached the point where they would turn back north. Their entire route from Blue Lake, which sat northeast of Bad Guy Headquarters, had made a wide circle around it so they could approach from the south. According to the plan, if the enemy fell for their ploy of taking refuge at Blue Lake, they would never look for them to come from that direction.

Now, as that last turn approached, a hubbub erupted ahead. A band of about twenty Bad Guys was tramping through the forest on some evil errand, prattling loudly as they went. The Good Guys took cover behind a cluster of bushes.

"I don't know what the Old Man is keeping the little scum for," said one Bad Guy. "Feeding him and everything."

"Yeah," said another. "If it was up to me, I'd fix him."

A third said, "I wouldn't have him in a nice, cozy room, eatin' our food and drinkin' our water. Let him starve, I say."

"They claim the Old Man's got some use for him, but if you asked me, I'd find a good use right now."

"Maybe we'll all have a good show one of these days. How would you like that, boys?"

They raised a round of rude cheers and laughter followed by more similar talk. The four Good Guys waited until the clatter faded into the distance before crawling from the bushes.

"I suppose what we just heard was good news, despite the way it was delivered," said Keith.

"I'd like to 'little scum' them," squeaked George, his tiny fists balled up tightly.

Marc Monster patted him gently on the back with one huge finger. "At least we know we are not too late, little friend."

They took long drinks from their canteens and were preparing to move on when the forest darkened. A check of the sky, or as much of it as they could see through the trees, showed a dark wall of clouds advancing toward them, a wall that had just swallowed up the sun.

Marc Monster sniffed the air. "Big storm's a brewin'," he said.

"It looks like you'll be going back into your plastic bag pretty soon, George. I know you'll love that," Keith said.

"Oh, for joy. I'd rather take on those jerks," said George, and he demonstrated some fancy footwork and punches.

Keith and Marc laughed at that, but in the midst of it the Lugu stopped them. "Shh, someone's coming."

They crawled back into the bushes. Flashes of movement and color among the trees confirmed his words, but whoever followed them moved with much more care than the rabble they had just encountered. The four prepared for a fight as the Lugu whispered, "They seem to know we are up here."

Someone pushed a branch aside, and they saw a face. It was Rick's, and Todd's was right behind. Rushing out, they pounded their friends' backs. Marc Monster picked up Todd and spun him around while embracing him in a bear hug.

"Now for the last leg…together," said Keith. Even as he spoke, the wind burst upon them.

All that day they had yearned for even the slightest rustle of air to take the edge off the oppressive heat, but it had remained as still as a Bad Guy's conscience. Now a whole day's worth of wind blew in a minute. A distant rumbling grew louder by the second, and soon the sky, now completely blackened with heavily laden clouds, flashed with blinding light all around. Todd plugged his ears against the deafening cracks that followed each flash and against the howling of the wind in the treetops.

"This is crazy," Keith shouted, trying to raise his voice above the storm. "We have to find cover."

A sandy bank tucked against a hillside offered the best shelter around, and they dashed to it, flinging themselves tightly against the sand wall. Plugging their ears against the all-too-frequent and all-too-nearby lightning strikes, they prayed that no trees close to them would draw a bolt or blow over. Although the bank gave them some protection against electrocution, it gave very little refuge from the rain. It filtered down through the leaves at first, drop by drop, but it quickly turned into a cloudburst as if the whole world were taking a cold shower. Where just minutes ago they sweltered, they now shivered in the chill of the wind and rain.

The lightning eventually moved along to the east, but the rain continued. Rick and Keith signaled the others to rise and resume the march. Everyone was drenched (except for George), and they trudged miserably along behind the leaders. The thunder no longer crackled, but they still heard a constant rumble. Its rolling growl, the rain's pounding, and the gusting wind made communication difficult.

Feeling completely wretched, Todd again thought of home and the comfort of roof, walls, and windows to protect him while watching storms. How exciting they had seemed from such cozy surroundings. Even Hairy Jack had his tin roof. Todd imagined how the drumming rain must sound on it. He saw, not far off the trail, a gigantic oak tree laying flat on the ground. It appeared to be hollow with a large cavity inside. He yelled to Rick, "We could probably crawl in there until the rain quits."

Rick looked at the tree and shouted back, "It might hold a couple of us but not everyone. Besides, we're as soaked as we're going to get already."

Keith added, "Anyhow, this might be a good time to travel. The Bad Guys will likely be holed up for the storm, so maybe it's the best thing that could have happened."

With a last wistful look at the tree, Todd followed along. Just before he turned away, something caught his eye. Had he just seen movement inside the hollow tree? Maybe some animal had taken cover there. Maybe a bear. "Thank heavens I took Rick and Keith's advice," he said to himself.

Not long after, the rain slackened and ceased as quickly as it had begun. The leaves still dripped, however, and the sodden underbrush sprinkled its collected water on any who brushed against it. Puddles dotted the trail, and rivulets ran hither and yon across the muddy ground. The temperature had dropped considerably.

Marc Monster dropped back next to Todd. "Once we dry out, we'll feel much more comfortable."

Todd hoped that would be soon.

Ahead of them, Keith grimaced and shook his head. Yes, they would be more comfortable, but they would be in grave danger. Very shortly they would reach Bad Guy headquarters, and their desperate mission would be made or broken. He tried not to think of what being broken would mean.

Chapter 15: Harsh Lodgings

Once Unexpected Hazards took custody of Mark, he took steps to prevent any further escape attempts. After giving his careless troops the "Proper punishment," he took Mark to a small room near the center of headquarters. The only light in this locked room came from a window with iron bars crisscrossing it like a tic-tac-toe board.

Among Unexpected Hazards' most trusted warriors were the group called his henchmen. Slip, Slide, Scratch, Cut, and Bruise, Mark's original captors, were henchmen. So was the first Bad Guy called on to be Mark's head guard, a grossly obese brute named Torture. Torture was fond of sitting on his victims, and his arms and hands, though blubbery in appearance, had the squeezing strength of a python. Mark remembered earlier encounters with Torture, and when the overstuffed villain jammed his pig-like face against the bars, Mark recoiled.

"Either you sit tight in your room, or I'll sit tight on you." Mark did not relish that possibility, and he sat meekly on the cot in his room.

Two more henchmen—Mark heard Torture call them Fracture and Injure—joined Torture shortly after his duty began.

After glaring menacingly at Mark, the three went into the main hall and sat down to play a card game that Mark guessed was some variation of poker. He could tell when each hand ended as two voices launched into streams of angry cursing while the other laughed derisively. From hand to hand, the pattern never changed, just the combination of voices.

It did not take Mark long to tire of this card table etiquette which was not quite the word he would have used for it. He tried to block it out by thinking of an escape plan or by reminiscing about better times. He tried to do some exercises and stretches. He hoped and prayed for help.

That night, three more henchmen relieved the first guards. The chief of them walked to the barred window and looked Mark up and down. Mark saw a pale, bloated, saggy face staring at him. Deep-set eyes, like muddy water at the bottom of twin pits, scanned him. A mouth full of rotted teeth grinned humorlessly, and a green tongue licked chapped lips. Random patches of bare skin shone red and inflamed amongst the greasy swatches of hair on the henchman's head. He scratched at them with clawed, scab-splotched fingers as he threatened Mark in a low voice. "Don't get too comfortable in there. You should know me, but they call me Papa Disease, and me and Abrasion and Laceration here don't put up with no guff. Orders is all that's keeping us away from you as it is, but don't tempt us."

The new set of guards spent the next few hours telling each other wicked and hurtful stories until they fell asleep. Mark sought a way to get out of his cell, but the lock held fast. After some time, he fell into a fitful sleep. In his dreams he saw an open gray sky above him that burst, sending a great deluge across the land.

He awoke to a familiar voice. "How ya doin', folks?" it asked. Mark jumped from his bed and pressed his face against the bars, joy rushing through him. The Lugu stood in the hall. But when he looked closer, his spirits fell. This looked like his friend. In fact, he would have struggled to tell them apart at any distance, but this was not his Lugu. Mark could tell that he was older, and the smile he was accustomed to seeing looked more like a leer.

"I see our little friend is waking up," said this Lugu. "You boys can run along now. I'll see to it that he stays put."

Papa Disease, Abrasion, and Laceration yawned, stretched, and filed out, glowering at Mark as they went. The Bad Lugu strolled over to the window, and Mark backed away.

"You wouldn't be confusing me with my wimpy nephew, would you? Well, don't. It insults me, and when I get insulted, I get mad. You wouldn't like that. My twin brother was a fool, and his kid ain't a whit smarter. Some day we'll get him just like we done my brother." He went into the hall and returned with a mug and two pieces of bread. He passed it through the bars to Mark. "It ain't my idea. If it was up to me, I wouldn't do it, but the Old Man says we have to feed you a couple of times a day."

Mark looked the bread over. After picking several spots of mold off the crust, he gulped it down. It was the first meal he had eaten since breakfast the day before. The mug contained water, warm but apparently clean. He poured half down his throat and set the rest aside for later. "Thanks. You're not so bad for a henchman," he said.

The Bad Lugu scowled at him. "You're gonna make me mad. I'm *not* a henchman. I'm the Old Man's right hand man, and don't you forget it. I told you not to insult me. Now give me the mug."

Mark hastily drank the remaining water and passed the mug through the bars. The Bad Lugu grabbed it and smiled sweetly, or as sweetly as possible for him. "By the way, my fine young friend, if you're counting on your buddies to come rescue you, you can think again. They're hiding out with their precious dinosaur friends. Isn't that just like a Good Guy? Enjoy your stay."

He walked away laughing.

They'd never do that, Mark assured himself. *Would they?*

So it went for Mark. He got another serving of bread and water that day and two again the next. He also got constant servings of insults, threats, and reminders that his friends had deserted him. As each day got hotter, so did his little room. The water never quite quenched his thirst. All the while, his guards responded to his suffering with mockery and derision.

On the fourth day of his captivity, Mark sensed that the Bad Guys had something big in the works. All morning they wandered in and out of headquarters in groups large and small. The buzzing among them sizzled with excitement, but Mark could not catch enough of any conversation to pinpoint why. A fear for his safety grew. Whatever they had in mind would not be good.

Chapter 16: The Fearsome Foursome

Early that afternoon, during Torture's guard duty, Unexpected Hazards himself strode in, followed by four others. Mark recognized them immediately. Gregory Ghost and Joe Giant were well known to all Good Guys. So were Bill and Barney Banshee. (While we normally think of banshees as wailing female spirits who foretell death, male banshees take on a more human form with personalities that tend toward one extreme or another—they are either sympathetic and caring or cruel and bloodthirsty. Bill and Barney fell into the second category.)

Possessing strength neither in body nor mind but an abundance of hatred and malice, the four were usually assigned to tasks that required neither of the former qualities. So inept were they that the Good Guys had sarcastically nicknamed them the Fearsome Foursome. Their bungling had turned the tide to the Good Guys' favor more than once.

Unexpected Hazards signaled to Torture, Fracture, and Injure, and they gathered with the Fearsome Foursome in front of Mark's door. "I want you three to come with me for our practice raid on those deserted cabins on Arrowhead Lake this afternoon,"

Unexpected Hazards said to the henchmen. "Then, of course, you will be coming on the big raid up north tonight." He glanced at the Fearsome Foursome. "All of my dependable troops will be there."

He turned to the Foursome. "In the meantime, I have an important job for you four. I want you to watch the prisoner. I don't care what happens. Just keep him locked up. And don't harm him. We need him in one piece for the time being. Can you chuckle-heads handle that?"

Bill Banshee answered with a sneer. "You can count on us, just like always. The fat kid won't have a chance with us on guard."

Unexpected frowned and shook his head. "Just keep him locked up," he said, leading the others outside.

Mark rubbed his hands across his lean stomach. *Fat?*

Bill Banshee pressed close to Mark's window. "Ya hear that, kid? Don't be giving us any lip. Ya try anything, and we'll fix ya."

"You won't have me for long. Rick and Keith will…."

"Haw, haw, haw," laughed Gregory Ghost. "Big generals, ha! And you, you, you couldn't even pass private. Haw, haw, haw."

Mark looked him in the eye. "I'm a captain. What are you?"

Gregory backed off, his eyes turning to the wall. "Shut up, kid. This ain't about me."

He led the others into the next room, and Mark retired to his cot. He heard a television set come to life, and he heard the Foursome arguing about the channel. They finally settled on a professional wrestling telecast. The four howled and cheered.

"Get him!"

"Jump on him again!"

"Break his leg!"

"Bang his head some more while the ref ain't lookin'!"

"*I* could fix 'em both!"

The match ended. Mark heard the announcer interviewing the winner. The Fearsome Foursome laughed heartily.

He heard Gregory Ghost's voice. "Big wrassler, ha. He's trying to talk like us."

Barney Banshee piped up, "If there's one thing I can't stand, it's a puffed up, loudmouth wrassler."

The bell rang to start another match, and the shouting resumed. Mark lay back, plugged his ears, and closed his eyes. He tried to ignore the heat that was becoming unbearable. He had just dozed off when Bill Banshee came to his window.

"The Old Man sent ya something to eat. I think it's a waste of food, but maybe he wants to keep you around for a while." He handed Mark the mug of water and watched him drink half of it. "Here's your food, ya fat kid. We got to worryin' about ya, thinkin' maybe it was poisoned, so we tasted it to see if it was safe. Rah, ha, ha." He tossed a couple of crusts through the bars before returning to the others, chortling as he went.

Mark picked up the crusts and dusted them off. He almost gagged at the thought of eating from the same bread as the Fearsome Foursome, but he knew he needed to maintain his energy, so he forced the crusts down. He glimpsed motion along the wall. Lifting his feet off the ground, he watched as a rat skulked out and nibbled at the crumbs.

"I got it first," Mark said, "Now git!" The rat scurried to the corner and squeezed through a hole in the wall. Mark wished that he could do the same.

From the TV, Mark heard the chattering of a dolphin. The four were watching a rerun of an old show about a boy who had befriended it. Once again, Mark's guards shouted at the screen.

"Kill the fish!"

"I hope the fish eats that fat kid first!"

"If there's one thing I can't stand, it's a smart aleck fish!"

Mark yelled at them through his bars. "That shows how stupid you are. A dolphin is a mammal, not a fish."

The Fearsome Foursome stormed out of the television room and crowded around Mark's door. Behind them, a skeleton pranced to a doorway and leaned against it, watching quietly.

"Shut up, ya fat kid," snarled Bill Banshee. "If we're so stupid, how come we have you locked up?"

"From what I recall, you had nothing to do with my being here," Mark replied.

"No," said Gregory Ghost, "but the Old Man picked us to watch you because he wanted his best boys on the job."

"Never send a boy to do a man's job," Mark snapped back.

Joe Giant made a huge, but flabby, fist and shook it in front of the window. "You little ostrich feather," he said. "Wait'll I get my hands on you. I'll fix you."

Bill Banshee joined in. "Ya fat kid, *I'll* fix ya."

"Wait a minute," said Mark. "You know the Old Man ordered you to guard me but not harm me. He might not like it if you 'fixed' me."

"Big deal, you little ostrich feather. It won't make much difference if I just rough you up a little."

Mark looked at Joe Giant in mock fear. "Hold on. You guys are such great fighters that you would probably kill me without even trying. Oh, I wouldn't risk it if I were you."

Bill Banshee intervened. "The fat kid's got a point there. You know how mad the Old Man gets at us sometimes. The fat kid'll be screamin' for mercy soon enough. Come on, boys. Let's see if a shark can kill that fat fish."

As they left, Barney glared at Mark and said, "If there's one thing I can't stand, it's a kid."

Through all of it, the skeleton stood in the doorway, watching intently. Now it sauntered past Mark's cell, saying as it passed, "Obese stripling. I shall repair you."

From down the hall, the calls of "Kill the fish!" resumed.

Some time later, Bill Banshee came to check on Mark and to pick up the mug. "I hope ya like our cookin', ya fat kid. Just don't be askin' for ice cream later, 'cause ya won't get it. You're skinny enough already, so ya better eat what ya get."

"Listen, I don't expect to be here long enough to get all that hungry. Rick and Keith will probably be along to get me any time now."

"Ha. Those fat Good Guys are hiding out somewhere. They don't give a rip about you."

"I wouldn't be so sure of that. If I were you, I'd help me out of here before they arrive."

"Why should *I* help *you*?"

"To save yourself a lot of trouble. When they find out that you four heroes were picked to guard me, they will likely go right for you."

"As if I was scared of them, the fat generals."

"You ought to be. You wouldn't stand a chance with either of them."

"They'd better not come around here, or they'll have to deal with me."

"They would deal you aside like a playing card."

"Quiet, kid, or I won't wait for what the Old Man has in store for you, fun as it may be."

"If he depends on you to do it, I'll be having all the fun."

"Oh, yeah? Well, I'll show *you*, ya fat kid!" Bill roared as he unlocked the door. "You've opened your mouth once too often, kid, and now you're gonna be sorry. I never seen a kid yet I couldn't fix."

He took a great, looping swing at Mark who ducked and heard the banshee's fist slam into the wall behind him. Charging into Bill Banshee, Mark flattened him onto the cot where he pinned him and pummeled him with punches.

"Help me! Help me! Help me!" screamed Bill Banshee. "Don't hit me no more. I'm already dead."

Hearing the commotion, the other three ran into the room and pulled Mark away from Bill. Bill stumbled up and launched another punch that glanced off Mark's forehead. Bill howled in pain. "You've had it now, ya fat kid. That was the hand you made me bang into the wall."

The other three laughed at him but held Mark fast. Normally, Mark could have overcome the whole group, but weakened by the heat and lack of food, he submitted to them. Bill Banshee slumped out of the cell, holding his injured fist.

"We're sick of listening to you," said Gregory Ghost. "The Old Man said to keep you locked up, but he didn't say where. Come on, boys. We'll lock him in the shed."

"But," said Joe Giant, "the Old Man said to keep him locked up."

"You idiot, I said we'll *lock* him in the shed."

Bill, Barney, and Joe dragged Mark outside while Gregory ran to get a padlock. They threw Mark into the shed, and Gregory snapped the lock. "You can babble all you want out here, and nobody will have to listen to you," said Joe.

As Mark fell onto the shed's wood floor, he saw something interesting above him. He waited until the sounds from the Fearsome Foursome faded. He tugged at his sweat-stained shirt and

wiped the perspiration from his face. Gathering all his strength, he
rose to his feet.

Back inside, the Fearsome Foursome sat in front of the television.
The reception, perfect earlier, now flickered with occasional static.
Joe Giant poked his head out the door. "There's a big line of clouds
coming in," he said. "Looks like rain."

　　Bill Banshee snickered. The snicker built until he shook with
laughter. "That oughta fix the fat kid," he managed to say.

　　"What do you mean?" asked Joe.

　　"I mean the fat kid is going to get soaked," he gasped
between loud guffaws. "Don't you remember the roof of that shed
rotted off a couple of years ago? He's gonna get doused like crazy."

　　The Fearsome Foursome barely saw the rest of their program
as they chortled without ceasing. By the time the program ended,
they heard the first roll of thunder.

Chapter 17: The Fearsome Foursome Fried Again

Mark surveyed the shed. His first impression had been how light the inside was, especially since there were no windows. Upon seeing the missing roof, his heart leapt. Trash and rubble lay strewn about the floor. Dragging and piling the debris to the back wall, he built a platform against it, pulled himself over, and dropped to the ground.

The air hung heavy with heat and humidity, but after the closeness of his room in enemy headquarters, it felt as fresh as a plunge into Blue Lake. More rubbish and filth littered the ground around the Bad Guys complex, but by the time he reached the woods beyond, he reveled in the beauty of the outside world.

He knew he must get his bearings straight before setting out. He did the best he could to estimate where the sun shone behind the oncoming clouds. That would be west. South would be a quarter-turn to the left. He hustled off in that direction, keeping a wary eye out for pursuit.

A distant rumble of thunder made him jump. He hoped the storm would track to the north or south, but as the clamor grew and

separated into distinct crashes, he knew otherwise. The imminent
danger of lightning drove him to seek cover. By the time he
found it, he was a half-mile or more from headquarters. The wind
picked up, and he feared for trees toppling on him. One such tree, a
huge oak ruined in some previous squall, offered the haven he
sought.

Even as the first bulbous drops of rain splattered on his back,
he crawled inside a gaping hollow space in the oak's trunk. Inside
he stayed dry, although he had to evict a small lizard and several
spiders. He felt safe and cozy as the storm pounded the forest
around him.

Shortly after the thunder's mightiest peels abated, he half
imagined he heard voices. Could it be a posse of Bad Guys in
pursuit of him or might it be some wandering raiding party? He
crawled deeper into the trunk, but in the process his right foot
slipped on a rotten chunk of wood and, for an instant, kicked out
near the opening. He prayed that no one saw it.

Several minutes passed, and nothing happened, nothing
except the slackening of the storm. Now the rain sprinkled down
lightly, and the thunder dwindled away into the east. Mark crept out
and breathed deeply of the cooler, dryer air. He raised his arms to

capture the refreshing breezes. Then he resumed his flight, south through Bad Guy country toward home.

The Fearsome Foursome chuckled and wisecracked about Mark's plight throughout the storm. Gregory Ghost bragged unceasingly about his brilliant idea, although the others insisted that they should be given part of the credit. "We'll probably get promoted for this," Gregory crowed.

Unbeknownst to them, a second storm was percolating. Unexpected Hazards and his practice raiding party straggled back into headquarters in a foul mood. The storm had cut their afternoon foray short. Drenched, dripping bodies shook with rage at scouting for booty missed or at least delayed. Then Unexpected Hazards checked on Mark's cell.

Bottles and glasses throughout headquarters trembled at the wrathful wail that followed. Unexpected Hazards bounced up and down, stamping both feet on the floor each time. The walls echoed with objects being thrown against them. His arms waved furiously, and everybody around him backed away. He stomped into the television room, his body stiff, his teeth clenched, and his eyes on fire. Had he held a weapon at that moment, the story of the Fearsome Foursome may have ended abruptly.

He stopped and glowered at each of the four in turn before saying in a cold, controlled voice, "Where is he?" When no one answered, he redirected his question at Bill Banshee. "Where is he?"

Bill shuffled his feet and looked Unexpected Hazards directly in the knees. "It's okay, boss. We've got the fat kid locked up."

"And just where might he be?"

Gregory Ghost, mistaking Unexpected's calm voice for forgiveness, interrupted, "He's locked up, boss, and this is rich." He chuckled, and a sneer formed on his lips. "He's in the old shed, and he's probably soaked more than you…uh, even more than you can imagine."

"In the old shed, eh? Lugu, check it out."

No one spoke from the time the Bad Lugu left until he returned. "He's gone, boss. Probably climbed out the roof. It rotted away, you know."

"It rotted away. I know," said Unexpected, slowly. The pitch of his still calm voice rose with each word. "Now tell me. Whose cockamamie idea was this?"

The Fearsome Foursome looked all around the room. They swallowed. They hemmed. They hawed. They twitched and shook. Gregory Ghost twiddled his thumbs behind his back. Then he answered. "It was their idea. I tried to talk them out of it, but they told me to shut up."

"Shut up!"

"He's lying."

"He did it."

"We had nothing to do with it."

The other three all spoke at once, each saying these four things, more or less. Unexpected Hazards raised his hand, and they all went silent, all except for Joe Giant, who was looking at Gregory. "You said the Old Man would probably promote us."

"The Old Man? The Old Man?" screamed Unexpected. The words that followed have no place in a book of this nature. Rest assured that he did not particularly appreciate the nickname. Upon completing his tirade, he barked one more word. "Sit!"

The Fearsome Foursome shuffled to the nearest chairs and meekly sat down. Unexpected went outside for several minutes. The others stood mutely in their places. When he returned, with regained composure, he fired out orders.

"Slip and Slide, I want you to get Scratch, Cut, Bruise, and Percy Scarecrow together and go after the kid. Bring him back. The rest of you, get the troops together. Even if he gets away, he will never get back in time for anyone to do anything about our plans for tonight. We're still going, all except for some of the goblins. Lugu, pick a dozen or so of them to hang around here for security. Now, get cracking."

The Bad Guys in the room pushed and shoved to the doors. Gregory, Bill, Barney, and Joe rose to follow. "Not you four. Sit down," said Unexpected. "You like watching TV? Make yourselves comfortable."

The four rearranged themselves to face the set. Bill and Barney flopped down on a dilapidated couch with springs sticking out everywhere. They looked at each other curiously. Unexpected walked to the wall and unplugged the set.

"How can we watch it if you do that?" asked Joe Giant.

Unexpected Hazards gave no reply. Instead, he dragged a chair over from the side of the room. He positioned it in front of the television, facing the Fearsome Foursome. "Just wait," he said, and he walked out.

The Fearsome Foursome resumed their bickering until Unexpected Hazards reappeared in the doorway, scowling and tapping his foot.

Moments later, Proper Skeleton entered the room, a smug look on his face. Sitting on the chair, he crossed his legs, opened a book, and read:

"Venerable, matronly sorceress

Descended violently into a roadside depression,

Elevated the most diminutive denomination of

coinage,

And assumed she was affluent."

Chapter 18: The Best Laid Plans

Rick, Keith, Todd, Marc Monster, and the Lugu drip-dried in a hidden spot a quarter mile from Bad Guy headquarters. George sat on his flashlight, enjoying the fresh air. With the storm retreating into the east, they prepared to fulfill their operation.

"We may as well eat now," said Keith. "Family Rooster is supposed to fly over in less than an hour, and then we need to be ready."

In their plan, Family Rooster would fly in a great circuit, returning to check on the six of them every fifteen minutes. Just before making their move, they would signal him. He would then fly to each group of Good Guys to mobilize them to meet the retreating rescuers and escort them home.

Marc Monster looked at the spots of sky visible through the trees. "The trick will be for him to see us through the leaves," he said.

"You've got a good point," said Keith as he half-munched and half-slurped a soggy wafer. "We may have to split up. Then, if he sees any of us, we'll let each other know before he comes back."

Everyone agreed, but Rick insisted upon taking Todd with

him. Marc Monster offered to carry George, who would be too small to be seen. The meal finished, they split up and agreed to meet in the same place in an hour.

The Lugu found a likely spot, open to the sky above but surrounded by thick brush on three sides. He crouched in a corner of it, a nook screened off from the fourth side by tall swamp grass, and waited, his eyes glued to the sky. Those eyes grew heavy, aching for sleep after the last night and day's journey. He struggled to stay awake.

Then he saw something, a speck in the sky. Was it the Family Rooster? Yes, it was. He saw him clearly, and he was about to fly right over his head. *But,* he thought, *will he see me?* The Lugu dashed into the clearing and waved his arms feverishly. He wanted to shout, but he did not want enemies to hear him. *He's going to miss me!*

Family Rooster had nearly passed the clearing when his head turned, and he dipped his wing to show the Lugu that he had seen him. He circled once and passed over the tree line.

The Good Lugu raised his arms triumphantly. Checking his watch, he saw that the Rooster should pass over twice more before the end of the hour. He sat back in his hiding place, shaking with excitement. The most dangerous part of the quest lay just ahead. He relished the thought of action. Soon Mark would be safe.

Family Rooster knew his orders and knew the strategy. Flying low above the trees to give the Bad Guys less chance of seeing him, he would patrol the region south of their headquarters and watch for his friends below. He worried about being spotted by the Bad Guys. He worried about missing his friends. And he worried about one thing more than any other—despite careful planning, he had forgotten what the signal would be.

He cruised above the treetops for some time before spotting something below. What was it? It looked like, yes, it was the Lugu. He was waving, signaling. And to think that he had almost missed seeing him! *So, they were going in already.* He banked to his left and sped away southwards.

The appointed quarter hour came, but Family Rooster did not. Nor did he appear on the half hour. A nervous Lugu made his way back to rejoin his friends and relate what he had seen.

"This isn't good news," said Rick. "I'm afraid something might have happened to him. I know he was clear on the plan."

"Then we'd best move as soon as possible," Marc Monster said. "I know he'd never spill our plans if captured, but…well, I guess they might get suspicious of him flying around the area."

"As soon as it's dark," said Keith.

The Lugu led them to his spot, where they huddled in the fading light, ever hopeful of Family Rooster's reappearance. Rick and Keith went over the plan with them until the first stars peeked out.

"It's time," said Keith.

With butterfly-infested stomachs, they entered the forest and sneaked the last quarter mile to headquarters. "Try not to rustle any branches or step on any sticks," Rick whispered to Todd. An owl hooted, and a colony of spring peepers began their evening chorus, but the travelers advanced with hardly a sound.

At length, they saw a chink of light between the trees. Bad Guy headquarters loomed ahead. Light shone from one window, but the bulk of it stood dark and apparently deserted. Staying just inside the trees, they skirted the compound until they reached the dark side. They inched forward, their ears and eyes alert for sentries or the ever-present debris hidden in the overgrown grass, waiting to trip them up. They reached the main building. Crouching now, they felt their way along the wall until they found what they sought, the fuse box.

Marc Monster held the dark flashlight up to the box, and George hopped out. Touching George's shoulder, Marc lifted his face to George and whispered, "Good luck." With that, George plunged into the fuse box and disappeared.

Todd heard his heart beating as he knelt still on the ground, waiting for George's return. His breathing sounded like a great wind, it seemed. *How long would this take?* He thought he heard a sound on the roof above. It was probably just a tree branch scraping across it. His heart skipped a beat when he saw that the others were looking up as well.

A mist seemed to pass over the stars, and in that same instant they were enmeshed in a tangle of rope. A face poked over the roof's edge.

"Got 'em!" a voice yelled, and then it exploded into ugly laughter. Crude cheering broke out from around the corner. The goblin on the roof raised his hands to celebrate, causing him to lose his balance and tumble squarely onto Marc Monster. Marc tried to grab him, but with every move he became more and more entangled.

The goblin rolled free. "I told you boys I could handle a net," he said.

The other goblins descended upon the Good Guys and bound them with stout rope before they could get oriented. "Well, what have we here?" said one. "Bring them in, boys, and we'll see what we caught."

With many a jerk and tug, the goblins hauled them into headquarters, snickering and whooping whenever a Good Guy stumbled. Every so often a goblin scampered up to them and delivered a kick before retreating just as quickly.

Once inside the lighted room, the goblins recognized their captives. Goblin voices buzzed with excitement. A large goblin pushed his way to the front. "This is a bigger prize than we had before," he said. "I think the Old Man would like to hear about this right away. Whetstone, you're the fastest. Go catch up with them and let them know. Get going." A tall, skinny goblin raced out of the room.

The large goblin circled the captives, cackling and rubbing his hands together. "Not quite as smart as you were in the forest the other day, are you? I suppose you thought you'd rescue your little friend," he continued in an oily tone. "You must have thought we wouldn't be watching. Maybe you could walk in here and walk out as you please. Probably rob us to boot." Now his voice turned hard. "Well, you can't. We've got a place for you."

The goblin pointed down the hall to a door with a barred window and a key protruding from the lock. It was the door to the very room where Mark had been imprisoned. Before taking their new captives to the room, the goblins took some time to gloat.

"You came skulking onto our property and got caught," the leader said. "Caught like rats in a trap. Ha, ha. Yes, rats in a trap, rats in a trap, rats in a trap," he chanted.

The other goblins picked up the refrain, and soon the room reverberated with it. "Rats in a trap. Rats in a trap. Rats in a trap." On and on they went, sneering and gesturing in mockery. "Rats in a trap. Rats in a trap."

Behind them, the door flew open with a crash. The goblins turned to look, and their chant died in their throats. Into the room stormed the fierce figure of Hairy Jack.

Hairy Jack's fury had been building from the moment Todd locked him in his own jail. Fishing for the keys took a long time, but patience paid off, and finally they slid down the stick to him. He had seen Todd leaving Gooseberry toward the south, and he remembered trouble coming to him from that direction in the past. He also remembered from whom it came. Without a minute's delay, he loped down the trail toward Bad Guy headquarters…and revenge.

He had jogged along for quite some time and had not even noticed he was hungry until he heard a tempting sound, more tempting than any fast food jingle. "Rats in a trap," it said.

Rats. *Yum!* In a trap. *How convenient!* His stomach growled, and his mouth slobbered. Vengeance could wait. Supper came first. "Rats," he gurgled.

Throwing the door open, he saw no rats, only a swarm of those cursed goblins. How he hated them! He waded into their midst, swinging wildly. Goblins flew this way and that. A handful of them ran to hide in Mark's cell.

Against the wall, the Good Guys struggled in vain with their ropes. Todd sat aghast at seeing Hairy Jack again. "We don't have a chance," he whispered. Then he saw something drop from the ceiling.

George leaped from the light. He ran in and out among the legs of the flustered goblins until he reached the Lugu. Pulling and tugging, he managed to untie the knot holding the Lugu's hands. Together they untied the others. The Lugu held out the flashlight, and George climbed inside. Edging carefully along the wall, the whole group reached the door unnoticed by Hairy Jack who was intent on goblin bashing.

"Where's Mark?" Rick whispered to the flashlight.

"I don't know. He's not here," came a high-pitched voice from inside.

Rick's mouth dropped. *What could this mean? It could be very good news. It could be very bad.*

Watching Hairy Jack rout the goblins, Keith whispered, "We're not doing him any good standing here." With that, they slipped out the door and darted for the cover of the woods.

Inside, Hairy Jack herded the goblins ever closer to Mark's cell. Forcing the last one in, he slammed the door shut and pulled out the key. In the room behind him, he saw several unconscious goblins. Carrying them one by one to the door and unlocking it each time, he chucked them in atop their terrified mates until the room was as packed as a phone booth full of fraternity brothers. He dropped the key on the table in the next room and walked out. He was satisfied, ready to go home.

"Rats in trap," he growled with a chuckle as he trotted into the forest.

Unexpected Hazards had been anticipating the massive raid for some time. The night was here, he thought, and no one could stop him. When Whetstone Goblin arrived, gasping for breath, he wanted to dismiss him until later, but the goblin persisted. At last, Unexpected agreed to listen, and, as he did, a wicked smile grew on his lean face. Here was news so exciting, so unbelievably delicious, that he forgot about the raid immediately. To have several of the top leaders of the Good Guys in his custody, that was a pretty piece of luck. He halted his troops and marched them, double time, back to headquarters. He sang a merry, but nasty, little tune as he marched beside them.

The tune changed abruptly when he found a sardine can of a room full of goblins. The raiding party instantly changed to a pursuit squad. As for the goblins, they were left to enjoy a little recital. It began like this:

>
"Adieu, infant lightly contacting a spheroid with the
>   express intent of advancing a base runner.
> Pater has adjourned to a Nimrod-like pursuit
> To procure a diminutive lapin epidermis
> To engulf the infant lightly contacting a spheroid with
>   the express intent of advancing a base runner."

Chapter 19: The Flights

Mark followed the most direct path home that he could, given the dark and the unfamiliar territory. Having put at least two miles between himself and Bad Guy headquarters, his hopes grew with each step. Now, however, he heard someone approaching from behind, running, if his ears served him right.

"Maybe it's Good Guys," he said to himself, but to be safe, he crawled into a thicket and waited. When the runners reached him, he saw they were no friends of his. He could not see well in the dark, but he recognized two or three of his original captors. They trotted past, huffing and puffing and making a clatter. From that time on, Mark advanced with utmost care, expecting an ambush at any time.

His stomach growled, begging for food, but he dared not search for any. He thought of the tasty meals awaiting him at his grandparents' house. At least he was able to take advantage of numerous springs in that soggy land, so he did not thirst. By moving slowly and deliberately, he thought, he could preserve his strength for the long hike home. Mosquitoes plagued him, as well. He did his best to brush them off, not wanting to risk the sound of slapping.

He progressed in short spurts. Scanning each tree and bush, he moved ahead only after assuring himself that no foe lay hidden in his path. Such a strategy made for slow going in the wee hours of the night. Once, he was on the verge of moving when a silhouetted motion caught his eye. Someone sitting in a tree shifted positions. Mark's breath caught in mid-inhale. Circling wide to avoid the tree, he thanked himself for his caution and vowed to redouble it.

Some time later, a cry that sounded like "breek, breek, breek" startled him and sent him on another wide detour. It was only a heron nesting along the shore of a nearby lake. The chattering of a squirrel sent him out of his way again. It was only scolding a skunk out on its nightly roving.

Farther along, the booming rush of a partridge spooked from its nest in an explosive launch into the air made his spine spasm in alarm. This time, he diverted his path all the way around a small pond. Had he known that Bruise, sneaking through the underbrush, had frightened the bird, he would have felt the full value of his wariness.

The rest of his night passed in much the same way. Somewhere between four and five in the morning, the day's first light glimmered on the edge of the eastern horizon. As it grew, Mark navigated more easily. When the sun had been up for about two hours, he saw its light flooding into a break in the forest ahead. Poking his head from behind one of the last trees, he saw the dam. He had reached the river and the border of Bad Guy Country.

With a glance to the left and right, he stepped out of the trees, crossed a road, and trotted to a fishermen's trail that led to the rocky riverbed below the dam. He was close now, so close that he could almost smell the bacon and eggs cooking, almost hear Grandpa and Keith's dad finishing the morning milking, almost taste a glass of orange juice. He felt the wind racing up the course of the river and into his face. He saw the path ahead and knew that it led to all these good things and to safety.

He paused for a moment to digest it all. Just as he placed his first shoe on the path, he heard a voice from the trees somewhere down the road. "Where do you think yer going, Sonnyboy?" Percy Scarecrow charged from the woods, and Mark plunged down the trail.

Rick, Keith, and the others ran on through the forest for over a half-mile before stopping to catch their breath and to consider their options.

"If he wasn't there, it must mean he escaped," said the Lugu.

"Not necessarily," Rick replied. "They may have moved him. They may have forced him to go with them on this raid the goblins mentioned. Or they may..." His words trailed off, and he left the rest unspoken.

"Well, we're just going to have to go back for him," Marc Monster said. "I can't bear to think of him being under their control for a minute longer."

Keith shook his head. "By the sound of things their big raiding party, apparently led by Unexpected Hazards himself, will be back soon, as soon as that goblin can catch them. Marc, we're good, but what could we do against their main force? Besides, the Lugu could be right. Mark may have escaped."

"He sure wasn't anywhere around there," said George.

Rick lowered his head and walked away from the group, back in the direction of headquarters. Marc Monster filled his lungs and curled both hands into fists. Rick stopped, stared into the woods for a minute, and returned. He looked each of his companions in the eye.

"Keith's right," he said. "If he did escape, we may catch up to him on our way out of here. If not, we may have a better chance of saving him by regrouping. I think we need to get back to our friends, and quickly. The Bad Guys will be on our tails any minute now."

Relief rushed through Todd's body. He had dreaded the thought of running back into the hornet's nest that Bad Guy headquarters would certainly be by now. An instant later, he felt selfish, and he longed to see his brother. As the group moved out, he was glad he did not have to make the decision.

Marc Monster heard the pursuit before anyone else. "They're after us," he cried, and he urged his friends to pick up the pace.

Todd looked to Rick. "How long before we reach the meeting point?"

"A long ways, even supposing Family Rooster made it through to our people. You'll have to push yourself. It's going to take everything you've got. You won't give up, will you?"

"No," said Todd in a strong voice, but he could only hope his body had the same determination. His breath was already short.

They sprinted through the woods, but in the dark they often stumbled on unseen objects. More than once, a marsh opening suddenly before them stymied their progress. Soon they all heard the pursuers. This was, after all, their enemies' country, and those enemies rushed confidently down paths that they had traveled hundreds of times. The Bad Guys also ran without fear. They could easily overcome the small group that had escaped from the goblins.

Marc Monster knew that the Bad Guys would soon overtake them. He saw Todd at his right, and he could tell that he was tiring. "You guys keep going," he said. "I'll stop and give them something to think about."

"Me, too," said the Lugu. "For my father!" He passed the flashlight to Rick and whirled with a growl.

At that moment, Keith, who was in the lead, saw someone waving to them far ahead. Whoever it was also called their names. "Keep going," he said to Marc Monster and the Lugu. "There are friends ahead!"

He led them forward in a final burst.

Chapter 20: Desperate Times

Family Rooster alerted the Bowdies first, since they lived closer to Bad Guy headquarters than any other Good Guys. When he told their leaders, Happiness and his sister Hope, that the operation had begun, they wasted no time. They mustered the Bowdy brigade and marched forth.

"They may need help before they get to the rendezvous point," said Hope. "Better to meet them as quickly as we can."

"Get reinforcements to the meeting place as soon as possible," said Happiness to Family Rooster.

So, while Family Rooster carried the word on to other groups, Happiness and Hope Bowdy left to intercept the rescuers. Following a route that they assumed their friends might take, they marched toward headquarters. They had covered a great distance when Happiness began to worry. His usually smiling face took on a concerned appearance. "They should have reached us long ago," he said.

Hope held his arm. "They'll find us," she assured him. "Many things could have happened, but they won't fail. They *will* find us."

As if to prove her right, they heard a tumult before them, the sound of many feet pounding the ground. They saw Keith; then they saw the others. As of one mind, the Bowdies waved their arms and shouted greetings. Keith and the rest reached them and fell breathless into their arms. In the next second, the vanguard of the Bad Guys appeared.

The Bowdies sent up a tremendous cheer. They waved swords and shook branches. The Bad Guys pulled up short. This was not in their plan. Believing they chased a handful of Good Guys, this new pandemonium shocked them. The anticipation of an easy victory turned to doubt. Had they known it, they far outnumbered the foe ahead of them, but the dark and the energy of the Bowdies made them waver.

Unexpected Hazards gathered his chiefs. "They're still too far from home. Just stick with 'em, boys, and we'll have a better look see sooner or later," he said.

The Bad Guys stood their ground but did not attack. When Happiness and Hope led the Good Guys away, Unexpected kept his forces a safe, but constant, distance behind.

For their part, the Bowdies followed a route that kept them in the woods, avoiding any clearings where their enemies might get a closer look and determine their numbers. Occasionally they stopped and created an uproar. Each Bowdy seemed to make the commotion of a dozen. Each time, the Bad Guys stopped as well, biding their time.

By and by, Hope spread the word, "The rendezvous is ahead."

Mark skidded and skittered down the trail. Under normal conditions he figured his chances of standing and fighting Percy alone would be good, but now, half-starved and weary, he decided his best chance was to flee. If he could only cross the river and gain the woods beyond, he might be able to elude Percy long enough to reach Vermillion Falls. *He'd never follow me there. Not in broad daylight*, Mark reasoned.

He made for the edge of a pool where the rocks formed a path of stepping-stones across the water. He heard Percy behind him.

"You won't get away from me this time, Sonnyboy. And you'd better not give me any trouble. Accidents have been known to happen."

Mark looked back and saw that Percy had already reached the trail. Despite his head start, Mark, usually a swift runner, saw the scarecrow gaining on him. He reached the pool and hopped to the first rock.

"Be careful you don't fall in, Sonnyboy."

Mark kept going, but he felt himself struggling. The rocks did not seem to be that far apart, but each jump took a lot out of him. With several rocks still ahead, he heard Percy close behind. He slipped as he landed on a large, slanted boulder, and before he could move on, Percy was on it, too.

"Now I have you where I want you, Sonnyboy," he barked triumphantly. He reached forward, grasping at Mark's throat before he could leap again.

Happiness Bowdy called Rick and Keith to him. "There's a big hayfield ahead," he said. "It was recently cut, so it's wide open. The meeting place is on the other side. You two need to make a decision. If we cross it, the Bad Guys will get an idea of how small our numbers really are. Going around it and through the woods will add more than a half-mile to our distance."

"But if we cross it, we should reach reinforcements right away?" asked Keith.

"We *should*, but only if they got there," said Happiness. "It's a long trip for some of them. But Family Rooster did reach us some time ago."

Rick thought for a moment. "You say Family Rooster came to you early? That should mean he got to everyone else early as well. That would give them extra time to get there."

"So I say we go for it," said Keith.

Rick agreed. "I don't want to take any more time than we have to," he said. "I'm starting to sense that the Bad Guys are getting impatient back there. If it's one risk against another, let's go where we may get help."

They reached the field and gathered for a dash across it. At a sign from Rick and Keith, they broke into the open. Todd labored through the first fifty yards, and he wondered if he had the strength left to finish the crossing.

Hope Bowdy dropped back beside him. Putting her hand on his shoulder, she said between breaths, "You...can do it. You are...a real...Good Guy now. Stay...with me."

Whether it was her encouragement, a rush of adrenaline, or the sound of the enemy firing into action behind them, Todd felt renewed energy. He focused on the woods ahead. He picked up speed.

Behind them, the Bad Guys roared with excitement. They saw only a small band crossing the field, an easy massacre. Their cruel, hateful cries rang in the open air and echoed in the trees beyond.

But was that an echo? Wait! The voices from the trees shouted encouragement. An army stepped out of them, not the entire Good Guy army, but a force large enough to challenge the evil at their heels.

The Bad Guys stumbled to a halt. Unexpected Hazards surveyed his forces. He surveyed the throng arrayed before him. A minute ago, easy victory appeared certain. Perhaps they could still vanquish the foe, but Unexpected was not looking for a fair fight. He wanted the odds in his favor. He cursed the Good Guys for ruining his plans, cursed his own soldiers for botching a good break, cursed fortune for turning against him. He wanted to destroy those who opposed him, to make them pay dearly. But not now. No, it would be best to get organized first.

"Let's get out of here, boys," he shouted, and the Bad Guys melted back into the forest as if by magic.

When Rick reached the far side of the field, he met the Gugu. "Thank heavens you made it on time," he gasped.

"Tha's all right," said the Gugu. "We've been waitin' here wonderin' when you'd be along. But you're here now. I guess it's time we're all movin' along. I brought your campin' equipment. Thought you might need it when you got home."

Mark steadied himself for the leap to the next rock, even while bracing for the backwards jerk that now seemed inevitable. Glancing back, he saw Percy reaching out just as he vaulted forward. He felt the fingers of gloved hands scrape across the back of his neck. *A narrow escape this time*, he thought. *Probably my last.*

Landing on a flat piece of granite, he heard a cry and looked back. Percy Scarecrow hung sideways in the air like a wide receiver undercut by a safety. Percy's legs kicked at the air. Beneath him flashed a fish, Ol' Red Gill himself. Percy splashed down hard in the pool. Ol' Red Gill hung balanced on the crest of the rock, his tail slashing furiously. At last, he tilted forward and slid into the river.

The old sturgeon swam past Percy, showering him with a heavy spray. He raced toward Mark's rock where he propelled his entire body out of the water. Was that a wink Mark saw as the fish passed before him? Ol' Red Gill reentered the water in a swish as graceful as an Olympic diver's. He jumped three more times on his way to the center of the pool, and Mark saw him no more.

Percy dragged himself coughing and sputtering to shore. As has often been said, there are none so slow as a waterlogged scarecrow. Percy had no chase left in him. He watched forlornly as Mark passed into the trees on the far bank. He limped back into Bad Guy Country leaving a wet trail, not unlike that of a snail, behind him.

"As far as the Old Man is concerned," he grumbled, "I never saw the brat."

Chapter 21: Homecoming

Mark trudged through Vermillion Falls, tired, hungry, but free. Joyously, ecstatically free. After one more short, weary walk, he would be back at Grandma and Grandpa's. One small problem nibbled away some of his joy; how could he explain his absence to the adults? Pondering this issue, he set out.

One event that Mark awaited with great anticipation each year was his first glimpse of the farm upon arriving from California. Today the sight of it delighted him more than ever before. As soon as it came into view, he summoned all his remaining strength and broke into a run. He did not stop until he threw himself onto the lawn where he caught his breath and let a torrent of tears cascade into the grass. Composing himself, he looked about the yard, the real yard and not a dream yard.

He entered the house and found his mom and Grandma finishing the dishes. "How was the camping trip?" his mother asked as if nothing was unusual.

Mark stared blankly for a few seconds before answering. "It was...fine."

Grandma looked at him. "You're all bit up. Didn't you use the mosquito spray? And just look at your eyes. Have you been crying?"

"I guess I forgot to put it on today. My eyes are just tired. You know, it's hard to sleep on these…campouts. I'm kind of hungry."

While Grandma went to get lotion for his bites, his mother got out a skillet and cracked two eggs into it. "Did you catch many fish?" she asked.

"A few."

"Who caught the most?"

"Rick, I guess."

"Good for him. Where are those other three, anyway? Should I be frying eggs for them, too?"

Mark was on the spot again. He took a long drink from the orange juice his mom had just handed him. "Uh, they'll be along later. They wanted to do some more fishing."

"I would have thought they'd have fished themselves out after four nights," said Grandma as she rubbed lotion on his many bites.

"Oh, you know them," said Mark. His mom placed the eggs and toast before him, and now he could use eating as an excuse for not talking. He followed the eggs with three bowls of cereal. When he finished, he mumbled something about taking a nap and rose to go upstairs.

Just then the door opened. Keith, Rick, and Todd stepped inside. "Done fishing already?" asked Grandma.

They answered by nodding but said nothing. They were looking at Mark, their eyes as big as his cereal bowl. Todd wanted to jump up and down. He saw Rick and Keith trembling, looking as if they would laugh or cry or both.

"You sure seem excited," said Rick's mother.

"Yeah, it was a great trip. We caught lots of fish," said Rick with a catch in his voice. "Keith caught the most. He must know the Wisconsin fish."

"But Mark said…oh, well, Mark said he was hungry. How about you three? And did you clean the fish?"

They nodded vigorously about eating, but Rick said, "We need to go upstairs and change while you cook it. And, uh, we released the fish. Come on, Mark."

They barely reached the top of the stairs when everyone burst into laughter and tears all at once. They alternately hugged Mark and pounded his back. Reaching Rick's bed, they all piled on it in spasms of joy. A small figure jumped out of a flashlight and joined them.

Grandma yelled from the bottom of the stairs, "You boys stop fighting."

After breakfast, Rick's mother said, "You'd better check down at the barn. Grandpa and Ben have three loads of hay to put up in the mow."

Rick, Mark, and Todd (who was too young to do much haying, but who came along nonetheless) went back upstairs to change into work clothes. Keith ran down to his house to do the same and to tell his mom about the "camping trip."

Gathering back at the barn, they found Grandpa sweeping the mangers and Ben washing the milkers. Ben greeted them and then said gruffly to Keith, "Not a very good time to go camping when there is hay to be made."

Keith smiled a guilty sort of smile and said, "Sorry, Dad. We'll all help a lot from now on."

Never one to stay gruff for long, Ben led the boys out to the hay elevator and to a full hay wagon next to it. "One of you can send the hay up, and two can mow it. I imagine you'll want Todd to be the boss." He winked at Todd. "You know, before we got the elevator I had to throw the bales up through the window. We'd have four or five guys up there mowing it, but I had to quit because they couldn't keep up."

He winked again to Todd who laughed and looked at the window, a good twelve feet above the ground. This was one of what he called the "Ben jokes," and hearing one again warmed him inside.

"Neat," he said.

Keith and Rick scrambled up the hay elevator. Mowing (which rhymed with plowing), or stacking, the hay could be a tricky business, and the itchy chaff glued itself to their bodies as they sweated.

They spent the rest of the morning working on the three loads, catching up on each others' adventures, and getting their "camping trip" stories straight. How good to be back on the farm, even if it meant working in a hot, dusty haymow.

That afternoon they finally got much needed naps. Awaking one by one, they worked up a game of plastic ball until time came to get the cows. They strolled out to the pasture together, laughing or commiserating as they recalled details of the last few days. At Buckwheat Hill, Rick told Mark about the meeting and the original plan.

The weather had turned comfortable after yesterday's storm. Cotton-like, angel clouds drifted across the sky. The day's high temperature was in the seventies, and the humidity had been washed from the air. As the four walked along the cow trail swapping stories, a soft, peaceful feeling engulfed them.

"What should we do tonight?" asked Keith.

Before anyone could answer, they heard a soft "psst" from behind some bushes. Satch Scarecrow poked his head out.

"Hey, Satch, haven't seen you since this morning. How's everything?" said Rick with a broad smile.

Satch smiled back, but his smile was not cheery. "I got some news from the scouts."

Keith wrinkled his forehead. "It's not bad news, is it?"

"Kind of. They said the Bad Guys are mobilizing. It looks like they'll be coming down for a fight tonight. According to the scouts, they're madder than a wet scarecrow."

Rick and Keith looked at each other, their smiles gone.

"Hmm," said Keith. "Can you get everyone together, all the groups? Have 'em meet right here at Buckwheat Hill tonight around dusk. And keep us posted on what the scouts find out."

Satch hurried back across the crick, and the four boys continued up the trail, the same trail that Rick, Keith, and Todd had started their quest on four nights earlier. Their carefree mood now turned somber. Deep thoughts replaced the light chatter from the first part of the walk. Coming to a point where the trail squeezed close to the crick, they heard a bullfrog's twang. Startled, Todd skipped to the side.

"It always does that," said Keith.

Little did he know how much that bullfrog would help.

Chapter 22: The Fight

That night the boys arranged to stay overnight at Keith's house. His mom prepared a typical hearty farm supper that included roast beef, potatoes and gravy, and pie filled generously with blackcaps, that is, black raspberries. After four days of short rations, the boys did not have to be asked twice when offered seconds, not even Todd.

They pitched in with the milking and other evening chores. Afterwards, while Keith's parents relaxed in the living room, the four of them organized for the coming attack. At sunset, Keith announced that they would be going out to study the stars and hauled out a star chart to prove it. Keith's mom told them to have a good time.

"Just be quiet when you come in. We'll probably be sleeping," she said.

The atmosphere at Buckwheat Hill that evening was as peaceful as the day had been, at least on the surface. The firefly display had only intensified over the last four nights. Early season crickets chirped their happy songs from their secret hideouts. The sound of leaves rustling gently from occasional puffs of wind could easily convince a person that all was right with the world.

Another sound, just a whit above a hush, soon reached the sharper ears. People, or beings, arriving in groups swished through the grass, filling the field gradually. Some, at signs from their leaders, concealed themselves in the trees around the field.

Rick and Keith kept mental counts of the groups as they arrived.

At last, Keith said, "Time to talk strategy." They, Mark, Todd, and a number of group leaders met atop the hill.

Satch Scarecrow brought the latest report from the scouts. "The Bad Guys are advancing in two divisions. Unexpected Hazards leads the first, and their Lugu leads the other. The Lugu's army is about ten minutes behind the first and seems to be taking a route farther to the west."

"Not the newest strategy in the world," said Rick, "but effective if we don't see it coming. It sounds like they plan to engage us in one direction and then hit us hard from the side or behind while our attention is on the first attack."

The others nodded in agreement. Keith asked, "How long until they get here?"

"Probably an hour and a half," said Satch.

Rick smiled grimly. "Then we have time to set a few things up. Let's hope that tonight's plans work out better than those we made the last time we met here."

Dark and silence continued to reign over the field, broken only by the flashing of the fireflies, the night sounds of insects, and the whispering of the leaves as the air flitted through them. When that air moved just right, the splash and gurgle of the crick below the field came to Todd, faint as an ancient memory.

Todd could almost hear his heart beating a dull rhythm. Clump, clump, clump, clump it went. Yes, he could actually hear it now, and it was growing louder. *Wait!*

That was not his heart. Footsteps approached. Many footsteps, the sound of feet on the march, approached, and the noise grew.

Clump, clump, clump, clump.

Now, he felt his heart beating faster and faster.

Clump, clump, clump.

The steps stopped. The quiet sounded worse than the tramping beat. Todd swallowed hard. His insides knotted up. He felt a trickle of sweat running down his nose. *Why was it so hard to breathe?*

The sound resumed, lower but closer. A band of bad ghosts and ghouls leaped into action and charged into a stand of white birches where they met opposition. The good skeletons held the birches, and the ghosts and ghouls retreated. No sooner had things quieted down than another party set upon a different grove of trees and were repelled in much the same manner.

"They're trying to lure us out," whispered Keith.

Rick pulled a pen light from his pocket, crouched behind a tree, and checked his watch. "Then I think it's time we gave them what they want," he said. He signaled to Marc Monster who blew a mighty, clear blast on a horn. Nothing happened.

"Thousand one, thousand two," an army of Good Guys counted.

They heard a babbling arise from across the way, but nothing happened.

"Thousand five, thousand six, thousand seven."

The babble rose to a clamor. Bad Guys jumped up and ran about, helter-skelter.

"Thousand ten, thousand eleven, thousand twelve."

Unexpected Hazards screamed for calm, but his troops struck at anything that moved. At that moment, the only things that moved were other Bad Guys.

"Thousand fourteen, thousand fifteen." With no further signal, the Good Guys burst from hiding. They smashed into the frenzied horde, driving it back like a rake through autumn leaves.

"Hold, you cowards, hold!" cried Unexpected Hazards, but even as he did so, he moved them back some fifty feet. He knew the second blow would not be as furious, and he knew he did not want to become fully entangled. Indeed, his forces could not match those waiting before him. Not yet. Keeping the Good Guys occupied was his goal for now.

"Hold, you milksops," he screamed, and he pulled them back fifty more feet. A sly grin flickered across his lips.

Chapter 23: A Lugu or Two

A few hundred feet up the crick, all still seemed calm. Wisps of mist rose from along the stream's course. When a bullfrog's twang broke the silence, one set of ears perked up. One body went into motion.

The Bad Lugu had blustered and bragged when asked to lead Unexpected Hazards' second battalion. From the moment he led them forth from headquarters, he had bullied and threatened his soldiers until he cowed them into following his every order. Now they marched along behind him, the first row exactly ten yards in his wake as he strutted toward battle, his chest puffed up nearly as much as his head.

A bullfrog croaking meant nothing to him but everything to his nephew who waited on the second limb of a great oak tree that grew at a sharp corner of the cow path. The bullfrog told him that someone was approaching. He had a strong notion as to who it was, too.

Peeping down through the leaves, he watched the Bad Lugu swagger past the tree and around the bend. As quickly and softly as a squirrel, the Good Lugu alighted from the tree just behind his uncle. He stepped out onto the path and raised his hand. The Bad

Guys obediently halted until he motioned them to their right. He led them down to the crick, across it, and up the far bank.

The bewildered Bad Guys glanced at each other, shrugged, and followed. They followed him through a pasture and around a field. They followed him through a pine wood, across a road, and over a longer field. They complied when he ordered them to line up three rows deep across the field.

"What in the blazes is he doing? I don't see no stinking Good Guys," growled one surly spook.

"Shut up and follow orders, you swine," said a skeleton next to him. "You know what the Old Man does to them that don't."

The Lugu raised his sword, and the army roared. It growled. It cursed. The field echoed with threats and insults. He lowered his sword, and the uproar ceased. He twirled the sword above his head and thrust it forward with a flourish.

With another bellow, the amassed multitude vaulted forward. Racing recklessly into the fray, it plowed full speed, wild in its fury…deep into the muck of a huge marsh.

By the time the drenched army pulled back, dripping with slime, swamp grass, and mire, its leader had vanished.

###

Meanwhile, the battle raged back at Buckwheat Hill. At least it would have raged had the Bad Guys not retreated with each advance of the Good Guys. Unexpected Hazards smiled to himself as he watched them concentrate their efforts against him. *So they think they are winning.*

When the Bad Lugu arrived, he laughed for Unexpected Hazards' plan and for his own cleverness. The unprotected backside of his enemies' forces stood before him, unaware of his presence. He twirled his sword about his head and thrust it forward with a flourish. He charged at the Good Guys with a shriek, a solitary figure hurtling into battle.

He had nearly reached their lines when he noticed an absence of shrieks behind him. Sliding to a halt, he whirled around and discovered his situation. He dropped his sword (without a flourish) and charged twice as fast in the other direction. He still shrieked, but with a different tone.

Word spread quickly through Good Guy lines. "The Lugu succeeded." Now there would be no more cat-and-mouse game. They rushed forward, and the Bad Guys could not retreat fast enough. The enemy bolted hither and thither for the north woods. Someone knocked Unexpected Hazards to the ground in the confusion, and he howled, "Hold me up, you ninnyhammers! Hold me up!" Torture grabbed him by the arm, and they joined the disorderly flight.

The Good Guys cheered as their foes disappeared into the night. Handshakes, hugs, and backslaps broke out everywhere. Rick, Mark, and Todd joined in the celebration.

"Great job, Keith!" shouted Rick, but Keith was not there. His eyes searched the field for his cousin but in vain.

"Over here!" someone shouted. Rick ran to the spot and found Hope Bowdy standing over a still body. To his horror, he looked down and saw Keith's unconscious form. Rick dropped to his knees and examined him. He found no wounds, but he saw a dark substance staining Keith's arm.

Recoiling, Rick called for help. "It looks like giant's blood," he said.

Family Rooster swooped in from the fringes of the battle, carrying Friendly Doctor on his back. Friendly Doctor nodded gravely. He cleaned the blood off Keith's arm, taking great care not to come in direct contact with it.

Hope Bowdy, who had seen the blood instantly, returned from the crick with a canteen full of water. Friendly Doctor took it and soaked four towels, wrapping Keith's head and body in them. He forced a foul-smelling liquid into his mouth. Then he waited.

Mark, Todd, and a number of others wandered over to where Keith lay. They sat quietly, watching the procedure. Todd whispered to Mark, "What's wrong?"

Mark answered. "You never saw the effects of giant's blood, did you? It's terrible. Poisonous. He could die." He saw the fear in Todd's face. "There's a good chance he won't, though. We found him right away."

Todd jumped when he heard Keith moan. The moan soon became an expressionless chant. "Giant's blood, giant's blood, giant's blood." On and on it went.

The Good Guys' cheering faded, first among those closest to Keith and then farther in all directions, like the ripples when a stone splashes into a pond. Concerned Good Guys gathered around Keith.

"Giant's blood, giant's blood, giant's blood."

Rick and Mark sat by, ready to aid the doctor at any time. The minutes passed with no change. Todd lost track of time. One hour? Three?

At last the chant ended but was quickly replaced by furious thrashing. Now Friendly Doctor, Rick, and Mark held Keith down. "He could hurt himself," Rick explained to Todd. "He needs to go through this stage, though."

Hope Bowdy kneeled next to them. "Don't worry, Keith. It will be all right. You will be fine. Relax. Be calm," she spoke in a soft, soothing voice. She continued in the same way until the thrashing stopped.

At long last, sweat trickled from Keith's forehead. The trickle turned into a torrent, and his clothes were drenched in it. Friendly Doctor drew a deep breath. "The worst is over," he said. "Watch over him until he comes to."

They kept vigil over Keith while the doctor helped others mend their wounds. All around, Good Guys were busy clearing the battlefield. With the night half gone, Keith sat up. Good Guys of all ranks filed by to wish him well. The Lugu came last.

"How ya doin', folks?" he said. He told everyone about his part of the battle. When he finished, Marc Monster told him about Keith. He led his friend toward the cluster of Good Guys gathered around the still woozy general.

A smile flickered across Marc's face. "I'm so happy you're doing better," he said to Keith, "because I can finally laugh."

He did, long and heartily, and so did everyone else, especially Keith.

###

At four in the morning, the boys sneaked to bed at Keith's house. They were quiet and woke no one.

Chapter 24: Life Goes On

Keith's head had barely dented his pillow when his dad woke him to get the cows for the morning milking. Pushing himself weakly to his feet, he felt his body aching from the exertions of the last few days and nights. His head spun from the lack of sleep and the aftereffects of giant's blood fever. He forced himself to dress and dragged himself out to the pasture.

Young bodies, however, bounce back quickly and soon regain their energy. By the time he finished the early chores, Keith felt ready to resume his normal life. He anticipated a full night's sleep at the end of this day. Even better, his vigor flowed back into him at the thought of spending the day with his cousins, all of them, in activities of their own choosing.

Rick, Mark, and Todd joined him for a long, leisurely breakfast of eggs, bacon, toast, and cereal. Mark looked at his toast and found no mold. His cold juice tasted delicious. Todd enjoyed a bowl of Sugar Honey Crunchies. As he savored its sweetness, he paused and set his spoon down. Just for a moment he yearned for the fare at the Lugu's and at the dinosaurs'. Smiling to himself, he finished the cereal and asked Keith's mom for another bowl.

Later that morning, Keith and Rick helped Grandpa and Ben make three more loads of hay. They enjoyed the loading, as they bounced along on the wagon on a bright June day. It made up for the hot, dusty unloading and mowing that followed.

Meanwhile, Todd sat on his grandparents' porch reading a new book, *Zoolatracs in the Old Gelb Mine*, a gift Rick had presented to him just that morning. Mark crossed down to the river and picked his way upstream, seeking to thank a new friend.

That afternoon, the haying done, bookmarks placed, and friends thanked, they gathered the golf equipment and played a round together on Keith's course. I would like to tell you that they all played excellent golf, but in keeping with the commitment to truthful accuracy that is the spirit of this book, I will say that they had a great time filled with good humor and warm companionship. They laughed at their good shots. They laughed at their bad. They laughed at the crows quarreling in the branches. They laughed for joy at life and friendship and the green world around them.

They knew that their victory was only temporary and that Unexpected Hazards would be back with more mischief. Indeed, more adventures awaited them in the weeks to come, but not just yet. And that was enough.

###

In the northern forest, life also returned to its usual rhythms. Good Guys everywhere pursued their daily routines. Marc Monster, the Lugu, Gugu, and Cuckoo tended to their home, chickens, and cows. Baby dinosaurs played with their anky-banks, and Friendly Doctor spun stories for them. Dr. Rankato chugged along in his old pickup selling rat-tailed bowties, fish diapers, and toenail shiners. Ol' Red Gill savored the algae he gleaned from the rocks below the dam. In Gooseberry, Hairy Jack searched his cabin for rats and (Could it be?) dreamed of Carnegie Hall.

The Bad Guy armies had barely finished licking their wounds and, for a good share of them, drying the swamp water from their bodies when Unexpected Hazards summoned them to headquarters. All day long they limped in, grumbling and scowling whenever they thought the "Old Man" was not watching.

When all had arrived, he assembled them in a dell that formed a large amphitheater. Standing before them on a small, makeshift stage and keeping his face expressionless, he spoke. "Boys, this week we were presented with a number of excellent opportunities to bring our enemies to their knees. Thanks to all of you who decided to think for themselves, thanks to your total incompetence…."

Here his face twisted into a pained frown and flushed raspberry red. He gritted his teeth and struggled to compose himself. "Now, to show you how much I appreciate your efforts, to reward you as you deserve for the jobs you have done…" With each word, his voice grew more harsh and his scowl more menacing. If it were possible for steam to spout from ears, his would have resembled stacks of a locomotive. He stormed from the stage, cursing under his breath and clenching his fists.

A familiar figure mounted the stage and began to read aloud. He read for an hour or more, but he began as follows:

"Petite John Horner

Reposed in a niche,

Consuming his yuletide pastry.

He inserted an opposable digit

And extracted a fleshy fruit

And expounded upon his personal virtue."

That night, Rick, Mark, Todd, and Keith slept soundly, their world at peace. All around the yard the fireflies flitted and flashed. Somewhere a bullfrog croaked as a Jersey cow wandered by. The scent of new mown hay drifted through their window, sweetening their dreams.

Outside, the leaves on the great elms rustled in the night breeze, whispering this story one to another.

THE END

Also by Keith Pitsch

Verle the Squirrel Shoots for the Stars

Verle the Squirrel and the Legend of Creepy Hollow

Coming Soon

One Room on Hemlock

For more about Keith and his projects, go to keithpitschauthor.com

www.ingramcontent.com/pod-product-compliance
Lightning Source LLC
Chambersburg PA
CBHW060146130626
46556CB00006B/2515